"It's Really Hot," She Said, Tilting Her Head Back And Stroking Her Neck With The Tips Of Her Fingers. "Feels Like My Skin's On Fire."

He inhaled slowly, deeply. She heard the deliberate intake of air, and it did her a world of good to know that he was totally affected by her.

"I gotta get back to work," he said tightly, and turned away.

"Oh, okay," Nora said. "I'll just go on inside and say hi to Emily, then."

He stopped. "You're staying?"

"Sure," she said, smiling. "We've still got to find me a man, don't we?" Then she spun around and walked toward the house, intentionally swaying her hips in what she hoped was a provocative move. She felt his gaze on her as she walked, and her skin hummed, her insides churned, her knees wobbled, and places in her body that had yet to be introduced to passion sat up and begged.

So just *who* was torturing *whom* here?

Dear Reader,

Revel in the month with a special day devoted to *L-O-V-E* by enjoying six passionate, powerful and provocative romances from Silhouette Desire.

Learn the secret of the Barone family's Valentine's Day curse, in *Sleeping Beauty's Billionaire* (#1489) by Caroline Cross, the second of twelve titles in the continuity series DYNASTIES: THE BARONES—the saga of an elite clan, caught in a web of danger, deceit…and desire.

In *Kiss Me, Cowboy!* (#1490) by Maureen Child, a delicious baker feeds the desire of a marriage-wary rancher. And passion flares when a detective and a socialite undertake a cross–country quest, in *That Blackhawk Bride* (#1491), the most recent installment of Barbara McCauley's popular SECRETS! miniseries.

A no-nonsense vet captures the attention of a royal bent on seduction, in *Charming the Prince* (#1492), the newest "fiery tale" by Laura Wright. In Meagan McKinney's latest MATCHED IN MONTANA title, *Plain Jane & the Hotshot* (#1493), a shy music teacher and a daredevil fireman make perfect harmony. And a California businessman finds himself longing for his girl Friday every day of the week, in *At the Tycoon's Command* (#1494) by Shawna Delacorte.

Celebrate Valentine's Day by reading all six of the steamy new love stories from Silhouette Desire this month.

Enjoy!

Joan Marlow Golan

Joan Marlow Golan
Senior Editor, Silhouette Desire

Please address questions and book requests to:
Silhouette Reader Service
U.S.: 3010 Walden Ave., P.O. Box 1325, Buffalo, NY 14269
Canadian: P.O. Box 609, Fort Erie, Ont. L2A 5X3

Kiss Me, Cowboy!
MAUREEN CHILD

Silhouette®

Desire.

Published by Silhouette Books
America's Publisher of Contemporary Romance

If you purchased this book without a cover you should be aware
that this book is stolen property. It was reported as "unsold and
destroyed" to the publisher, and neither the author nor the
publisher has received any payment for this "stripped book."

 SILHOUETTE BOOKS

ISBN 0-373-76490-1

KISS ME, COWBOY!

Copyright © 2003 by Maureen Child

All rights reserved. Except for use in any review, the reproduction
or utilization of this work in whole or in part in any form by any
electronic, mechanical or other means, now known or hereafter
invented, including xerography, photocopying and recording, or in
any information storage or retrieval system, is forbidden without
the written permission of the editorial office, Silhouette Books,
300 East 42nd Street, New York, NY 10017 U.S.A.

All characters in this book have no existence outside the imagination of
the author and have no relation whatsoever to anyone bearing the same
name or names. They are not even distantly inspired by any individual
known or unknown to the author, and all incidents are pure invention.

This edition published by arrangement with Harlequin Books S.A.

® and TM are trademarks of Harlequin Books S.A., used under license.
Trademarks indicated with ® are registered in the United States Patent
and Trademark Office, the Canadian Trade Marks Office and in other
countries.

Visit Silhouette at www.eHarlequin.com

Printed in U.S.A.

Books by Maureen Child

MAUREEN CHILD

is a California native who loves to travel. Every chance they get, she and her husband are taking off on another research trip. The author of more than sixty books, Maureen loves a happy ending and still swears that she has the best job in the world. She lives in Southern California with her husband, two children and a golden retriever with delusions of grandeur.

Visit her Web site at www.maureenchild.com.

One

Being a virgin wasn't all it was cracked up to be.

But then, Nora Bailey was about to change all that, wasn't she? The question was, just who could she find to help her get rid of her chastity belt? Pickin's were slim, as they say.

Staring out the gleaming front window of her bakery, Nora watched the citizens of Tesoro, California, enjoying a beautiful spring morning. With a calculating eye, she studied only the men walking along the crowded, narrow main street.

First, she spotted Dewy Fontaine, ninety if he was a day, heading into the pharmacy across the street. He stopped to say hello to Dixon Hill, father of six, working on his third wife. Nora shuddered.

Trevor Church raced by on his skateboard. Cute, but eighteen, for pity's sake. The kid popped a wheelie as he slipped around the corner and disappeared.

Harrison DeLong, sixty and just a little too spry, stopped to shake hands and kiss babies. Running for mayor...*again*, and who trusts politicians?

Mike Fallon. Nora sighed. Nope. Her gaze lingered on him for a moment or two as he strolled down the street toward the ice-cream parlor. Tall, he wore faded denims and a short-sleeved, dark red shirt. His boots were scuffed, his dark hair was ruffled in the breeze, and Nora knew, without even being able to see them, that his green eyes would be shuttered. Wary. Heck, the only female Mike trusted was his five-year-old daughter, Emily. Just then, the little girl raced up to her father and grabbed his hand with both of hers. Mike glanced down and gave his pretty daughter one of his rare yet breathtaking smiles.

A darn shame that Mike wasn't in the running.

"Wouldn't you know it?" she muttered. "I'm finally ready to 'do the deed' and there's no one left to do it *with*."

Way back in high school, she'd made the decision to remain a virgin until she was married. At the time, it had seemed like the smart thing to do. But she hadn't counted on being the only twenty-eight-year-old virgin in the country, for crying out loud.

She'd expected to graduate from college, find Mr. Right, get married and have babies. Pretty old-fashioned dreams, she supposed, in the grand scheme of things. But then, she'd been born and raised in Tesoro, a tiny coastal town in central California, where people still had bake sales to raise money for the school. Where neighbors looked out for one another and doors were mostly left unlocked.

Where single men were now harder to find than a calorie-free chocolate chip cookie.

So here she stood, eleven years after high school, as pure as the day she was born. The whole celibacy thing had really lost most of its shine. Nora had clung to her vow through the years, despite the fact that both of her younger sisters were married, with a baby each. She'd told herself repeatedly that the right man would come along. But honestly, she'd begun to doubt it lately. After all, she'd never been the kind of woman men lusted after.

Her sisters were small and pretty. Nora was tall, too forthright for her own good and stubborn to boot. She was terrible at flirting, too honest to play games and too busy building her business to kill time at bars or dance clubs.

But the kicker, the impetus to call this whole virginity thing off, had strolled into Nora's bakery only the day before. Becky Sloane was getting married. The kid Nora used to baby-sit had come in to order her wedding cake. A four-tiered, white chocolate number with pink and yellow roses. Becky—or rather her mother—was sparing no expense. At nineteen, Becky was on engagement number two, and Nora was willing to bet she hadn't said no to number one yet, either.

And that's when Nora first wondered just who she'd been saving her virginity for. At the rate she was going, she would be able to be buried "intact" and her headstone could read Returned, Unopened. Depressing. Which was why she was now so determined to leave the ranks of the pure and unsullied behind.

After all, just how much was a woman expected to take?

Naturally, she'd talked her decision over with her best friend, Molly, over lunch yesterday, mentioning her encounter with Becky Sloane.

"Becky Sloane?" Molly repeated, "I remember when the kid couldn't tie her shoe."

"I know. So how old does that make us?"

"God, how humiliating for you," Molly muttered, and took another long drink of the frosty concoction in front of her. "Becky's getting married and here you sit, as pure as the driven—whatever the heck that means—snow."

"Gee, thanks," Nora said. "I feel so much better now."

She winced. "Sorry." Green-eyed Molly Jackson's red hair was short and cut into a pixielike do with sharp edges and twisted curls that somehow looked great on her. Loyal to the bone, Molly was funny, impatient and creative enough to have launched her own greeting card company that she ran from her home. She also happened to be the mother of the world's cutest six month old girl and was married to the town sheriff, a man who absolutely adored her.

"When's the wedding?" Molly asked.

"Next week," Nora told her. "Saturday."

Two red eyebrows arched. "That's fast."

"Yes," Nora said, and twirled her straw through the slushy drink in front of her. "And honestly, Becky didn't look so good. A little green around the gills."

"Hmm. So maybe there's a reason for the big hurry, huh?"

"I don't know," Nora said. "But if Becky is pregnant, then that puts her way ahead of me, doesn't it?"

Molly smiled and shook her head. "This is a contest, then?"

"No." Nora sighed and leaned back in her seat. "It's just that I used to baby-sit her and now she's starting out on her life while I…"

"Bake a mean cinnamon roll?"

"Exactly."

"Well, you know how much I love to say 'I told you so,'" Molly said. "But I won't this time. All I will say is it's past time that you did something about this, Nora. You know darn well that most men avoid virgins like the plague. They figure virgins are too romantic. Too willing to build picket fences around a man."

"True."

So to find Mr. Right—if he existed—she needed to be rid of the whole virgin thing. Surely an experienced woman would have better luck.

From the back of the bar, an old jukebox blasted out sixties tunes. Along one wall, a row of booths with scarred red vinyl seats marched in a line. Each table held a candle covered by red plastic netting that was supposed to have added atmosphere. But, over the years, the patrons had peeled away so much of the netting that now the candles simply looked like they had acne.

She and Molly sat at a table on the far side of the room, hidden by the shadows and practically covered by the silk vines of trailing ivy plants hanging from pots overhead. A few regulars were sitting on stools at the bar while couples occupied the booths and snuggled in close together.

Nora sighed, tore her gaze away from the most amorous couple in the bunch and looked seriously at her friend. "What I have to do then is become an ex-virgin."

"Haven't I been saying that for the last five years?"

"You said no 'I told you so's.'"

"My bad." Molly held up a hand as if taking an oath and swore solemnly, "I will never again point out to you that you took so long coming to the conclusion that single, unattached males in Tesoro are almost extinct. Still, you're better off shopping at home. Who knows what kind of man you'd find in the city?"

Nora had to smile. If there was one thing in her life she could count on, it was Molly being absolutely honest with her. Even when she didn't want to hear it.

"Well, I feel better."

"You will," Molly promised as she finished off her margarita. "As soon as you get past this one little roadblock."

"Little?"

"Okay not so little. But we'll find you a man. You wait and see. I mean, it's not as if you're an old maid or something. Not yet, anyway."

Nora shivered. There was a horrible thought. She got an instant mental image of herself, forty years from now, living alone except for the dozen cats crawling all over her doily-covered furniture. Nope. That's not the life she wanted. She wanted a family. She wanted love. And it was high time she went out and started looking for it.

"I can do this, right?"

"Absolutely."

But before Nora could relax a little, Molly asked, "What's the time limit on this?"

"Time limit?"

Molly nodded. "I know you, Nora. If given half a chance, you'll talk yourself out of it. If we don't set a timer on this, you won't get moving. You'll end up sitting back and waiting for Mr. Right again."

"Do you really think there *is* a Mr. Right?" Nora asked quietly. She'd always believed there was someone for everyone. The older she got, though, the less likely that theory looked.

"Yeah," Molly said after a couple of minutes' thought. "I do." The soft smile on her face forced a tiny pang of—not jealousy, because Nora would never begrudge her best friend the happiness she'd found with Jeff—but maybe a little envy.

"How is your Mr. Right, anyway?"

Molly grinned. "Terrific. He's watching the baby down at the office." She checked her watch then and gulped. "And I'd better get down there and rescue him so he can get back to business. But before I go…time limit?"

"How do I know how long it'll take?"

"Uh-huh. How about three months?"

Nora thought about it. Could she really do this? Set herself out to trap some guy into helping her rid herself of what she'd come to think of as an albatross hanging from her neck? And if she didn't do it? Then what? Start shopping for cats? Oh, no. "Okay. Three months."

"Atta girl." Molly grinned. "Before you know it, you'll be living happily ever after, Nor. You wait and see."

A timer went off, ending Nora's thoughts about yesterday's conversation with Molly and bringing her back to the moment at hand. Hurrying through the swinging door into the kitchen, she snatched up a hot pad, yanked open the oven door and pulled out a tray of steaming cinnamon sticky buns.

She smiled as she set them on the cooling tray, then in a smooth, practiced motion, slid the next baking pan into the oven. As the scent of toasted pecans and warm cinnamon filled the room, Nora leaned back against the marble mixing counter and looked around the room.

Small but efficient, her little kitchen was outfitted with the very best equipment she could afford. She'd made a name for herself in Tesoro over the last few years. Her bakery was becoming so popular that she was even drawing customers in from Carmel and Monterey. Her business was thriving, she had a great little house just a block from the bakery and parents and two sisters she loved. All that was missing was a family of her own.

And that was a gnawing, constant ache in the bottom of her heart.

She'd always thought there would be time. During college, she'd been too focused on graduating to do much dating. And after graduation, she'd attended chef's school and pastry classes. Then she'd concentrated on opening her business. And once the bakery was open, it had taken every moment of her time to get it up and running and make it successful.

Now that it was, she had time to notice what she was missing. The years had swept by so quickly, she hadn't realized that most of the women she'd grown up with were married and had children already. And as her biological clock—God, she hated that phrase—raced on, her time was running out. She didn't want to be forty and just starting her family. Yes, it worked for a lot of women, she knew that. It just wasn't what she'd wanted or expected her life to be.

As much as she loved being Aunt Nora to her sisters' two little girls, it just wasn't enough. And if she was going to change the situation, she had to do something about it now.

There was one bright spot in all this. Everyone for twenty miles around would be invited to Becky Sloane's wedding. Surely she'd be able to find at least one single, available male there.

"For heaven's sake Nora, when was the last time you had a manicure?"

Nora snatched her hand free of her sister's and examined her less than perfect nails. "I've been busy. You know, working?"

"Nobody's that busy," Jenny snapped. She grabbed her sister's hand again and, scowling, began to file.

"What is up with your hair?" Frannie stared at her older sister in the mirror, her pale eyes reflecting an appalled fascination. "Have you been hacking at it with scissors again?"

Nora flinched and lifted her free hand to defensively smooth down the rough edges of her so-called "hairdo." "I resent the word, *hacking*."

"As a beautician, I resent what you did to your hair."

Her sisters. Nora sighed and looked at them. Petite and blond, the two of them looked like cheerleader bookends. Jenny and Frannie, at twenty-four and twenty-three respectively, had each married their high school sweethearts and were blissfully happy. Nora didn't begrudge either of them. But, as their older sister, she wouldn't mind having a little bliss herself. As close as twins, her sisters had always been a twosome. Pretty, popular and confident, they'd had the males of Tesoro eating out of their hands since kindergarten.

Now, Nora had never had any problem with self-confidence, either, but she'd always been more comfortable playing a sport rather than standing on the sidelines shaking pom-poms. And while her sisters used charm to sway opinion, Nora was more likely to argue a point until her opponent was simply too worn down to care anymore.

So why was she here in the tiny shop connected to Frannie's house, putting herself through this?

Okay, Nora told herself, maybe this hadn't been such a good idea, after all. She'd thought that the fastest, easiest way to whip herself into shape was to go to her sisters for help. But was the torture worth the end result?

"I can't believe you're finally letting me do your hair."

"Just don't get crazy," Nora warned.

Frannie snorted a laugh. "Don't panic. I promise not to introduce you to real *style*."

"Funny."

"Thanks."

"I think we'll do acrylic nails on you," Jenny said, clearly disgusted. "Your own are hopeless and too far gone to be saved."

Nora shot her a look. "Why not just cut my hands off?"

"I should. They're so chapped, it's a disgrace."

Okay, help was one thing. Sitting here being humiliated was another. Pushing herself up, Nora said, "That's it. I'm out of here."

Frannie held her down and caught her gaze in the mirror. "We promise to stop picking on you, but I'm not letting you out of my shop with your hair like that.

People will think I did it and my reputation will be shot."

"That's not picking?"

"Last dig, I swear."

"Me, too." Jenny's gaze met Nora's in the mirror. "Stay, okay? We'll make you so gorgeous you'll outshine the bride."

Nora eased back down, and as she did, the tension in the room dropped away and Frannie chuckled.

"That won't be hard. From what I hear, morning sickness may have Becky hurling all the way down the aisle."

"Her mother insists it's the flu," Jenny said.

"Yeah, a nine-month virus."

That comment sent Jenny off on more local gossip, and as her sisters' voices drifted around her, Nora closed her eyes and hoped to high heaven she'd recognize herself once her sisters were through working their "magic."

Two

Mike Fallon pulled at the dark blue necktie that was damn near strangling him and told himself that attending the wedding was good for business. In a town the size of Tesoro, it didn't pay to alienate any of your potential customers. Besides, he couldn't hide away on his ranch. He had Emily to think about. Whether he liked it or not, she would grow up. And he didn't want her to be known as the "hermit's daughter."

Though, God knew, if he had his choice, he'd just as soon stay out on the ranch as come into town and make small talk. But then, that was one of the reasons his ex-wife, Vicky, had divorced him, wasn't it?

Don't go there, he silently warned himself. Don't start thinking about Vicky and the mistake that had been their marriage. Hell, wasn't he miserable enough? He took a sip of beer, leaned one shoulder against a flower-bedecked wall and, to distract himself, looked out over the crowd wandering around the country club's reception room.

Almost instantly, his gaze locked on Nora Bailey. Now, *there* was a distraction.

His gaze swept over her, from the top of her perfectly done hair, down to the curves hidden beneath her sexy little black dress and right to the tips of her three inch heels. When he'd first caught a glimpse of her in the church, he'd had to do a double take. This was a Nora he'd never seen before.

He was used to seeing her standing behind her bakery counter, giving out free cookies to the kids and running her hands through hair that looked as though she'd taken her electric mixer to it.

Tonight, she was different. Mike's hand tightened on the beer bottle, and when he took another drink, he had to force the icy liquid past the hard knot lodged in his throat. Damn, she looked good. Her honey-blond hair was shorter and danced around her face in a mass of loose curls. Her dark blue eyes looked somehow smokier, and her legs were displayed to awesome perfection. Who would have guessed that beneath her usual uniform of apron, jeans and T-shirt, she was hiding such an amazing figure?

He watched her as she moved through the crowd, laughing, talking…*drinking*. Her steps a little unsteady, she tended to wobble, then catch herself as she moved toward him with the deliberately careful walk of a drunk trying to look sober. Frowning, Mike told himself it was none of his business if Nora wanted to have a few.

"Room tilting?" he asked as she came closer.

Nora stopped dead, lifted her chin and squinted to get a good look at him. She blinked and tried to clear her vision. But it was no use. Mike Fallon definitely had not one, but *two* gorgeous faces. And the harder she tried, the blurrier he got. At last, she gave it up.

Maybe she shouldn't have had that last margarita, she thought as a flush of heat swept through her.

"Hi, Mike." She blew out a breath. "And no, it's not tilting. Swaying a little, maybe." Narrowing her eyes, she looked him up and down. "I'm surprised to see you here."

"The whole town's here."

"Yeah," she said, shifting her gaze to let it slide across the crowd. Just as her sisters had predicted, the bride was a lovely shade of green. Becky's new groom danced attendance on her while her mother told everyone who would stand still enough to listen about the virulent flu her poor daughter had caught.

Except for the tasty margaritas, the night, as far as Nora was concerned, had been a bust. She hadn't found anyone willing to take her virginity out for a spin, so to speak. Still, the reception wasn't over yet.

Her gaze slid back to Mike. Even blurry, he was too handsome for his own good. His rugged jaw and deep green eyes really were fantasy material. And though she preferred him in his jeans and boots, a suit jacket looked pretty good on him, too. Good enough that she was willing to give it a shot.

Leaning in toward him, she smiled and batted her eyelashes.

"You have something in your eyes?"

"No," she said, and reared back to glare at him. "I was flirting."

"Badly."

"Gee, thanks."

"Nora, what's going on?"

She sighed and reached up to push her hand through her hair until she remembered that Frannie had sprayed it into a football helmet. Letting her hand drop to her side again, she muttered, "Nothing. Absolutely *nothing* is going on."

And, the way things were looking, she was pretty sure she was headed for that house full of cats.

"If you don't mind my saying so," Mike said softly, his voice just carrying over the rock and roll blasting from the speakers at the front of the reception hall, "you're acting a little...weird."

"Weird?" She put one hand on his chest and shoved. He didn't move. "*I'm* acting weird?" Nora laughed shortly. "You come to a big party and stand in a corner by yourself and *I'm* the one acting weird?" She shook her head and immediately regretted the action. "Whoa," she whispered. Then, when the room righted itself again, she continued. "You know," she said, taking a deep breath, "you can go to a party, but if you're not *at* the party, then you might as well not have gone to the party. You know what I mean?"

"Not a clue."

She huffed out a breath. Pointless to try to get through to him, she thought. And while she stood here talking to the statue that was Mike Fallon, she was missing opportunities. "Never mind. We are *so* not comoon-commuti—" she paused to corral her tongue around the word—"*communicating.*"

His lips twitched into what might have been a smile, but it flashed across his face and disappeared again so quickly, she couldn't be sure. It *was* a great face, she thought. Heck, even blurry, he looked good. "It's a shame," she muttered.

"What is?"

Nora shook her head and waved one hand at him. "Nothing. Nothing. See you, Mike."

She walked away then and his gaze dropped to the

curve of her behind. Hell, what man's wouldn't? It was a great behind. But Mike frowned to himself as he wondered what she'd meant by *it's a shame*.

Over the next couple of hours, he watched Nora laughing and talking with her friends, and a part of him envied how comfortable she was with people. Socializing had never come easily to Mike and he figured it was too late now to change that. Even if he'd wanted to.

He took a sip of his second beer of the night and realized it had gone warm. Setting it down on the table in front of him, he forgot about it and focused instead on the tall blonde in black. Strange, but he couldn't seem to stop watching Nora. Or thinking about her. He could have left the reception an hour ago. Ordinarily, he would have. But for some reason, tonight, he just wasn't ready to leave yet.

Bill Hammond, Tesoro's self-described ladies' man, moved in on Nora. When she threw her head back to look at him, Mike's gaze fixed on the elegant line of her throat.

Bill's gaze was focused a little lower.

"Nora," someone close by said in a deep voice, "you look amazing."

"Thank you." Actually, even she'd had to admit that her sisters' handiwork had turned out pretty well. Though she did have to fight the urge to pull down on her hem and up on her neckline. Before this, she'd never owned anything that exposed so much skin— except a swimsuit. Turning around to thank whoever it was talking to her, she smiled up at Bill Hammond and hoped he didn't notice her disappointment.

As the local ladies' man, Bill considered any single female between the ages of eighteen and eighty fair game. Getting a compliment from him was as special as seeing a snowflake in a blizzard. Still, she felt she was in no position to be choosy.

His dark brown hair was styled just right, his dark brown eyes skimmed over her in appreciation, then slipped past her, as if making sure there was no one more interesting around. A small part of her sizzled in annoyance, but she smothered it. Nora had come to the wedding with one thought in mind: find a suitable guy to help her out of celibacy.

And since Bill seemed to be the only one offering…

"Would you like to dance?" he asked.

Before her rational mind could react and tell him to go away, Nora spoke up. "You bet."

She stumbled slightly but told herself it was because her new shoes hurt her feet. Who on earth had ever decided women should wear high heels?

Nora swayed slightly, but, since she was dancing, she hoped no one would notice. Oh, she really shouldn't have had that last margarita. But she'd needed a little false courage to deal with this whole man hunt. Now that she'd actually caught a man's interest, she wasn't at all sure she was pleased about it.

Bill's hands seemed to be everywhere. Instead of being excited, Nora just wanted him to stop it. But she swallowed back the no she wanted to give him. After all, this had been the plan all along, right? Now wasn't the time to get nervous. Instead she told herself to get in the spirit of things.

He guided her into a turn around the dance floor, and the crowd surrounding them seemed to blur into a wash of color and motion. Yet, somehow, she managed to spot one pair of deep green eyes watching her from across the room.

Mike.

Her heart did a strange little bump and roll as she locked gazes with him. A moment later, that feeling was gone as Bill whispered, "Let's step outside for some fresh air."

Fresh air. That's probably all she needed. Good idea.

"Okay," she said, and walked beside him, the heavy weight of his arm draped across her shoulders as he steered her through the crowd and out the French doors.

Night air rushed toward them, cool and sweet, with the scent of the flower gardens just beyond the brick patio. Nora slipped free of Bill's arm and immediately felt lighter and more free as she crossed the patio and came to a stop at the river-stone balustrade.

She tipped her head back to look up at the sky, sprinkled with diamond-like stars. A soft sea breeze drifted past her, tugging at her hair, caressing her skin and even, she thought wryly, clearing away some of the haze in her brain.

Enough so that when Bill approached her from behind, she wished she were anywhere but there.

"Did I tell you that you look great tonight?" he asked.

"Probably."

"Well," he said, sliding one hand down the length of her bare arm, "just in case I didn't, I'll say it now. Man, Nora, I had no idea you could look like this."

Well, there was a backhanded compliment if she'd ever heard one. What did she look like usually, she wondered, a gargoyle?

"Thanks."

"You're just as sweet as one of your pastries."

She winced. Did lines like that really work?

"Now I want to see if you taste as good as you look."

And with that smooth come-on, he turned her around and stared down into her eyes with a hunger she'd never seen directed at her before. A deep, dark hole opened up in the pit of Nora's stomach, and for one shining moment, she thought for sure she'd be thoroughly and violently ill. Then Bill grabbed her close with all the sensitivity of a starving man reaching for the only steak left in the world.

Her hands flat against his chest, she tried to hold him off, but with his arms pinning her to him, it was useless. Her mind raced with a speed that surprised her, considering just how wobbly she'd been a moment before. How could she have allowed herself to get into this position? Heck, forty cats were suddenly looking pretty good.

Before she could do anything to stop him, his mouth was coming down on hers and all Nora could think was that she'd never noticed just how thick and wet Bill's lips were. She felt…nothing. No excitement. No anticipation. Not even fear or anxiety. Just a mild sort of revulsion that she was pretty sure she'd have to get over if she ever wanted to lose her "virgin" status.

"Let her go."

A deep voice. Close by.

Nora's eyes wheeled as she searched the dimly lit patio for the intruder. A second later, Bill was plucked off of her and effortlessly tossed to one side.

He staggered slightly, regained his footing and scowled at the man standing protectively close to Nora.

"Back off, Bill," Mike said.

"Who invited you into this?"

"I didn't have to be invited." Clearly disgusted,

Mike added, "Can't you see she's had too much to drink?"

"Mike…" Nora said, grabbing at his arm.

He shrugged her off, never taking his eyes off of Bill, who didn't look at all happy about having his romantic moves interrupted.

"This is between me and Nora."

"Ordinarily," Mike said, "I'd agree. Not tonight."

"Who're you?" Bill demanded. "Her father?"

She felt as though she were trapped in an old movie. Hero and villain were squaring off, with the heroine standing on the sidelines, wringing her hands. Well, she'd never been much of a hand wringer.

"Okay," Nora piped up again. "Why don't you guys—"

"Shut up a minute, all right?" Mike said, not even glancing at her.

"Shut up?" She glared at him and only got angrier when she noticed he was paying no attention to her at all. "You're telling me to shut up?"

He finally shot her a quick look. "Just sit down, will you?"

"Look, I don't need you to—"

"It's okay, Nora. This'll only take a minute."

But her protests came a little late as Bill suddenly charged. Mike stepped to the left, drew his right arm back and landed a solid punch to the other man's jaw. Bill did a strange, almost ballet-like spin and crumpled into the nearby shrubbery without a sound. Stunned, Nora stared down at her would-be lover, now sprawled in the well-tended bushes. She noted that music was still playing inside. The crowd was still celebrating. No one but she and the two men involved had any idea of what was going on out here in the shadows.

That was some consolation, she guessed. At least half the town hadn't witnessed this little scene.

Everything was ruined now. Her plan shot, she turned and looked up at the man who had inadvertently kept her a virgin one more night. She'd have had to have been blind not to see the flash of satisfaction in Mike's eyes. How very...male of him. Planting one hand in the center of his chest, she gave him a shove and was pleased to see him back up a little.

"What do you think you're doing?"

Clearly bewildered, Mike just gaped at her for a moment or two before saying, "I think I'm saving you from a jerk."

"Did I ask to be saved?"

"No, but—"

"Did I look scared? Panicked?"

"No," he admitted, pushing the edges of his jacket back to shove both hands in his pants pockets. "You looked a little disgusted."

"And that requires rescue?"

When he didn't say anything, Nora threw both

hands in the air and started pacing. Her heels clicked menacingly on the bricks, keeping time with her fury.

Mike watched her warily but had to admit that she looked good with the fire of rage in her cheeks. What she was so mad about, he hadn't a clue. Hell, he'd thought he was doing her a favor. Usually, Nora was sensible. Reasonable. Tonight, though, she hadn't been acting at all like herself. When he saw Bill steer her out into the night, he knew the man was about to make a play. And since Mike also knew that Nora'd had one too many celebratory drinks, he'd figured she might need a hand peeling Bill's hands off her body.

Of course, he hadn't counted on the quick rush of…something that had filled him the minute he spotted Bill Hammond draped across Nora's frame. And he didn't want to explore that feeling at the moment, either. Right now, he was more concerned with staying out of her reach.

"Three hundred dollars," she was saying. "Counting the manicure and the haircut—I mean, they're my sisters, but it's their job, right? They have a right to be paid. Plus the new dress—and I hate shopping."

A woman? Who hated shopping?

"What are you talking about?" His gaze followed her as she marched back and forth past Bill's prone body.

"This." She waved her hands up and down her body, indicating the whole package. "The dress, the hair, the makeup, these stupid, too expensive shoes that are killing me. Not to mention this purse. It's only big enough to hold my keys and my driver's license! How can they charge seventy-five bucks for that?''

"How the hell should I know, but—''

She cut him off again. "That's not the point, though, is it?''

No, the point was that he'd come out here to be a rescuer and she was making him feel like Typhoid Mike. He should have gone with his first instinct. To mind his own business. What was it his father used to say? Oh, yes. "No good deed goes unpunished.'' He could almost hear the old man laughing at him.

He folded his arms across his chest, bit down on the anger rumbling through him and said, "Why don't you tell me what the point is, exactly?''

"Fine.''

She stopped right in front of him, tilted her head back to look into his eyes and wobbled unsteadily. She hardly blinked when he moved quickly to grab hold of her upper arms to steady her.

"The point is,'' she said, "I had a plan. A perfectly good plan and you've ruined it.'' She half turned, looked over her shoulder to where Bill was just stirring and pushing himself out of the hedges.

Mike followed her gaze. "Bill was your plan?''

"Certainly a big part of it,'' she countered, then frowning, turned back to Mike. A drooping blond curl fell across her forehead and she blew out a breath, sending it out of her eyes.

Her cheeks flushed, her eyes dancing with impatience, frustration and anger, she made a hell of a picture. It was damn near enough to make Mike's mouth water. Which worried him enough to let her go and take a long step backward.

"Okay fine. Bill's waking up. I'll just get out of here and you can go back to your...plan."

Bill muttered under his breath, rubbed his jaw and slowly climbed out of the bushes. Once he was on his feet again, he gave Mike a hot glare, avoided looking at Nora altogether and headed back toward the reception. His steps were steady, but the greenery stuck in his hair spoiled his attempt at dignity.

When they were alone on the patio again, Nora threw her hands high and let them slap down against her sides again. "See? Ruined. Now I'll have to find someone else."

But apparently, Mike thought, not tonight, since she walked past him and started down the brick walkway that ringed the clubhouse. Faux antique lampposts lined the walk, dropping small puddles of light into the shadows. Nora walked unevenly, wobbling from one side of the bricks to the other. Mike glanced over his shoulder at the crowded room behind him, then back to Nora. No contest.

He caught up to her in a few long strides. She was moving slowly, carefully, and limping painfully.

"These things are killing me," she complained just before she kicked first her right shoe, then the left, into the ivy lining the walkway. She sighed in satisfaction and started walking again, leaving the hated shoes behind. Mike chuckled to himself, scooped up her shoes in one hand and followed, wondering what in the hell had happened to turn the ever-sensible Nora into a beautiful, exasperating stranger.

He was about to find out.

Three

Mike kept a wary eye on Nora as she moved farther away from the wedding reception, still in full swing just twenty feet from them. Her steps wobbly on the brick walkway, she seemed to sway through the puddles of light dropped by the tall lamps lining the path. The night air was thick with the scent of flowers, and the dance music from inside came muted and soft, like a delicate backdrop. Nora kept muttering under her breath, and though he couldn't make out what she was saying, the tone of her voice told him it was probably just as well. Shaking his head, he followed her, tucking her shoes into the pockets of his jacket. She probably wouldn't thank him, but he figured the best thing he could do now was to get her into his car and take her home.

Then she stopped suddenly, turned, and before he could react, she slammed into his chest. Staggering slightly, she lifted her chin, looked into his eyes and blinked, as if trying to bring him into focus. He knew the feeling. It was as if he were seeing her for the first time. Her blue eyes were dreamy and her skin looked like fine porcelain in the dim, soft light. A slight sea breeze kicked in from the ocean only a mile or two away, and ruffled her hair with a lover's caress. For one brief moment, Mike thought about pulling her close, slanting his mouth over hers and—

"This is your fault," she said.

He laughed, the romantic image he'd been building, shattered. "You drinking too much is my fault?"

"Not that." She waved a hand at him, scowling. "You're not paying attention."

True. He hadn't been paying attention to her words. He'd been too distracted by her curves. "Okay, now I'm listening."

She inhaled deeply, then let her breath out in a rush, ruffling the blond curl hanging over her forehead. He'd never seen her so...*loose.* Usually, Nora was friendly but businesslike as she stood behind her counter at the bakery. Tonight was a revelation in a lot of ways.

Frustration bubbled inside Nora. Not that she'd been

all that excited about being kissed by Bill Hammond. Actually, just remembering the feel of his mouth on hers was enough to give her a cold chill. But he had, after all, been the only man offering. She swiped one hand across her forehead, pushing that one drooping curl back into place, and as she did, her brain seemed to clear briefly.

"What was I thinking?" she muttered.

"Sort of what I was wondering," Mike said.

She looked up at him, grateful to see that he was just a shade less blurry than before. But blurry or focused, he was more than worth a look or two. And it wasn't just his good looks or forest-green eyes. There was just something about Mike. Something...solid, dependable. As sturdy as a brick wall and just about as funny. Mike generally wasn't much of a smiler. "Okay, fine, Bill was a mistake."

"Granted. The question is, why were you about to make it?"

Nora huffed out a breath. "It's not like I had a lot of choices, you know."

Mike shook his head. "I still don't have a clue what you're talking about."

"What I'm talking about is, you ruined the plan."

"*What* plan?"

"It's your fault," she said again. "You messed it up, so you owe me."

"I peeled a jerk off you."

"Exactly," she snapped, and narrowed her gaze on him as he swayed back and forth. "And stand still."

"I'm not moving."

"Oh, boy. That can't be good." She frowned at him. "Are you laughing at me?"

He held both hands up in mock surrender and shook his head, while managing to hide his smile. "Not a chance."

"You have to promise to help me."

"Help you what?"

"I'll tell you after you promise to help."

"I don't do blind promises."

"But you owe me."

"Stop saying that."

"Then promise."

Mike glanced around. Everyone else was still inside, but he didn't know how long that was going to last. Nora was still unsteady on her feet and her blue eyes were just a little hazy from too many margaritas. Plus, it seemed as though she was willing to stand here and argue forever. He figured the only way out of this was to promise to whatever it was she wanted. Then he could pour her into his car and take her home. Hell, she'd probably forget all about this mess when she sobered up, anyway.

"Okay, fine. I promise." Taking her arm, he steered her toward the parking lot again.

She pulled free.

Stubborn, he thought, and waited for whatever was coming next.

"Oh." She blinked, then smiled. "Well, good then. That's better." She reached out and patted his chest with the flat of her hand. "You are a prince among tides...no...a prince among...princes!"

"That's me. Prince Mike." He took her hand in his and tried not to think about the flash of heat that stabbed through him with that simple touch. It had been way too long since he'd felt the kind of electrical charge that was even now sizzling along his blood-stream. Hell, until that moment, he'd have been willing to bet his "lust-o-meter" was broken. But apparently not. Oh, yeah. Best to get her home fast. Best for both of them. She was too tipsy for him to be thinking what he was thinking. "Now, I'll take you home before you get into more trouble."

"I wasn't *in* trouble," she argued.

"Not what it looked like to me."

"Hey, you think it was easy for me, flirting with everybody in the room?" Nora pulled her hand free of his and poked him in the chest with the tip of her forefinger. "You think it's easy to pretend to be interested in how Adam Marshal tunes an engine? Or to look fascinated when Dave Edwards described his white-water rafting trip for the fifth time?" She sighed heavily. "And that's not even counting the times I had to hear the mayor practice his Founders Day speech."

"Sounds pretty bad."

"You have no idea."

"So why do it?"

She shifted her gaze to look out over the darkened clubhouse grounds. "Because I'm twenty-eight-years-old and the kid I used to baby-sit just got married."

"And that means..."

Disgusted, she turned her gaze back to his. "It means, that unless I make some changes, I'm looking at old-maidhood."

"Are you nuts?" Mike took a good, hard look at her. Every one of her curves was outlined to perfection. Her blue eyes flashed in the dim light tossed by the lamps overhead and her honey-blond hair shone like gold.

"Nuts? Probably," she said on a heavy sigh. "But this is *so* much worse. I am the last of a dying breed. A dinosaur. A...what else is extinct?"

"What the hell are you talking about?"

"I'm a virgin."

"A *virgin?*" Well, she had his attention now. He took an instinctive step backward, as if trying to keep a safe distance between them.

"Say it a little louder. I don't think the folks in the back row quite caught it." Then she laughed, but there was no humor in the sound as she studied his expression. "Ah, and there's the 'look.' Honesly—honestly...poker? Not your game. All of you guys react to a virgin like a vampire to sunlight." She turned her back on him and started off down the walkway toward the parking lot again, muttering with every step. "That is so like a man. Say the word *virgin* and he leaps out of the way as if a bullet's aimed at his heart."

"I didn't leap."

"Hah!"

Mike followed after her and when he caught up, he grabbed her upper arm and spun her around to look at him. Then he reached up, shoved one hand through his hair and tried to concentrate. But hey, it wasn't easy. He hadn't guessed there *were* any virgins over the age of twenty.

"You caught me off guard, Nora."

"Yeah," she said glumly, lifting her gaze to his. "It's a real icebreaker." Sucking in a gulp of jasmine-scented air, she continued. "Anyway, the point is, I was trying to find someone to help me with my…situation."

"Bill?" he asked, astonishment coloring his tone. "Bill's the guy you picked?"

Instead of answering that question, she asked one of her own. "I look pretty good, right?"

His gaze swept her up and down before settling back on her face again. "Oh, yeah."

"I'm reasonably intelligent."

"I thought so, until a few minutes ago."

She gave him a tight, un-amused smile. "So getting rid of my...*problem* should be fairly easy, right?"

He wasn't so sure about that. Speaking for himself, he wasn't about to get too close to a virgin. For her, sex would take on more meaning than it should. It would evolve into white-picket fences and family dinners and babies and—he slammed a mental door on his thoughts. No way was he going to get wrapped up in this. Nora was a nice-enough woman and, God knew, she filled out a little black dress better than anyone he'd ever seen before, but he just wasn't the man for her.

For anyone.

"Nora..."

"You said you'd help."

Panic reared its ugly head. "I promised to help," he qualified. "Not to—" He stopped talking and stared at her for a long minute.

But she wasn't listening. Stepping up close to him, she fisted both of her hands on his lapels and went up on her toes until she was looking directly into his eyes. "I don't wanna be an old maid. I don't wanna bunch of cats. I want babies. I want family. I—"

Even in the dim light, he saw her face pale and her eyes go wide and round. "Are you okay?"

"Oh," she said softly, letting him go and lifting one hand to cover her mouth. "I am *so* far from okay."

Nora's stomach rolled uneasily and she swallowed

hard, fighting for control. Deep breaths, she told herself, and tried to put that thought into action. But it didn't seem to be helping. Her head was swimming, and her stomach pitched and dived as if it were a tiny boat in the middle of a stormy sea. "Oh, boy," she muttered, concentrating on the misery sliding through her body.

"Maybe I should just take you home."

"Yeah. Good idea."

With his warm hand cupping her elbow, she focused on the heat of his skin to fight against the chills sweeping through her. Tipping her face back into the breeze, she pulled in several deep breaths and told herself silently that nausea was just mind over matter. Mind over matter. Mind over—

"Oh, God." She pulled away from him, leaned into the shrubbery and was thoroughly, violently ill. Her brain raced, pointing out all the ways she'd managed to humiliate herself on this one glorious night.

She'd flirted shamelessly—and badly. She'd allowed Bill Hammond, of all people, to kiss her. And, to put a cap on the evening, she was throwing up a lung in front of Mike Fallon. Oh, yeah. This had gone well. She might as well go buy her first starter cat.

Her big night of seduction had turned into a cautionary tale.

But as the spasms of sickness slowly passed, Nora became aware of a cool, dry hand on her forehead and the sound of Mike's soft, soothing whispers. As embarrassing as this moment was, she was glad he was there. The only thing worse than being sick in front of someone was being sick all alone.

Straightening up, she inhaled deeply and noticed that the haze in her brain was completely gone. It had been replaced by a pounding bass drum, but at least she could think and see again.

Mike handed her a handkerchief. As she took it, she smiled. "Thanks. I didn't think anyone carried these anymore."

He shrugged. "Just an old-fashioned guy, I guess."

And, apparently, a nice-enough guy to completely avoid mentioning her most recent humiliation.

"So," he said. "You still want that ride home?"

"Yeah. Thanks."

On the short ride to Nora's place, Mike studied her. With most of the alcohol out of her system, he was guessing she was beginning to regret telling him all about the whole "virgin thing." And frankly, he'd be just as happy to forget about it himself. As it was, he'd been doing too much thinking about Nora now that he'd seen her out of her jeans and into something he couldn't help imagining getting her out of.

Hell.

His fists tightened around the steering wheel and he told himself to just keep his mind on the road. To not think about the swell of her breasts above the low cut neckline of that dress. And, while he was at it, he really should keep the image of her legs out of his brain. And just to be on the safe side, he figured he'd start forgetting about the curve of her rear and the soft shine of her hair and—

Hell.

He steered the car down her street and barely glanced at the tidy lawns and picture-perfect houses as he drove down to the middle of the block. Pulling into her driveway, he threw the car into Park, cut the engine and turned in his seat to look at her.

Damn. Even in the shadows, she was way too pretty for his peace of mind.

"Thanks," she said, turning her head to look at him.

"Want me to arrange to get your car back tonight?"

"No," she said, opening the car door and stepping out. "I can walk into the bakery tomorrow and then pick up my car later."

Mike got out of the car and walked up the driveway, just a step or two behind her. She'd left the front porch light on and a soft, golden glow streamed from the Tiffany style glass shade and dazzled the small space with slices of color. He noticed some kind of flower trailing from a series of hanging pots and a short glider swing that was dotted with comfy-looking cushions.

Sort of made him curious as to what the inside of her house looked like. But it wasn't likely he'd be finding out. She might not want to think about what she'd said when the margaritas were doing her thinking for her, but he remembered it all.

She wanted love. Family. Babies.

And that was enough to convince him to keep his distance.

Nora opened her front door and more light spilled into the darkness, like a warm, golden path laid out to welcome him. This could be serious trouble.

"I'm going to make me some strong coffee," Nora said, looking over her shoulder at him. "Want a cup?"

Say no, his brain screamed. One last stab at rational thinking echoed over and over through his brain, and for some unknown reason, Mike vetoed it. "Sure."

He followed her inside and she shut the door behind him. Mike fought down the feeling of being a prisoner hearing a cell door slamming closed.

Nora walked past him and headed down a short hallway. Mike stayed right behind her, and when she hit a switch, he blinked at the bright light ricocheting off the kitchen's sunshine-yellow walls. A white pedestal table surrounded by four captain's chairs sat in front of a bay window. Plants lined the windowsills, and the gleaming countertops boasted an assortment of top-of-the-line appliances.

She moved around the room in her stocking feet as Mike watched her. Every movement was smooth, no motion was wasted. This was a woman who spent a lot of time in her kitchen. She seemed far more at home here than she had at that party.

Something they had in common.

When she had the coffee brewing, she turned around to face him. "I'm just going to go freshen up. Have a seat, I'll be back in a minute."

As she left the room, Mike glanced at the table and chairs and beyond the shining window panes into the darkness outside. A cozy setup, he thought, and told himself again he should be going. After all, Emily was at home with a baby-sitter and he had an early day waiting for him tomorrow. But, for some reason, he wasn't ready to leave yet. He told himself he was only sticking around to make sure she was all right.

But even he was having trouble believing that.

"Sorry I made you miss the reception," Nora called from the other room.

"No problem," he answered. "I'm not really much of a party guy."

"Well, duh."

He smiled to himself and took a seat at the table.

A few minutes later, Nora breezed back into the kitchen. She'd changed into a pair of denim shorts and a short-sleeved, deep blue T-shirt that clung to her body with the same tempting allure that black dress had displayed. Her legs looked long and lean and slightly tanned. Her bare feet were decorated with a silver toe ring on her left foot and pale pink polish on her toenails.

And Mike knew he was getting in deeper here every damn minute.

The coffeepot hissed and steamed, sounding like an old woman shushing a crowd. Nora pulled two thick yellow mugs out of a cabinet and poured them each a cup of coffee.

"You take it black, right?"

He arched a brow. "Impressive."

Nora smiled, sat down opposite him and pushed one hand through hair that now looked soft and untamed. "Hey, a good businesswoman remembers how her customers like their coffee." She took a sip, closed her eyes and said, "Let's see, you prefer the cinnamon buns and Emily loves my chocolate chip cookies and you come in every Wednesday afternoon when you pick her up from school."

He didn't know whether to be further impressed or a little irritated that he'd become such a creature of habit that a storekeeper could set her watch by him. When had that happened?

"So," Nora was saying, and Mike listened up. Already that night he'd learned that it was important to stay on his toes when she was talking. "You've seen me at my worst tonight, that's for sure."

"Nora," he said, fingering the handle of his coffee

cup, "why don't we just forget about everything that happened and—"

"No way."

"What?"

"You heard me," Nora said, leaning back in her chair to give him a slow smile that damn near set fire to his insides. "You promised to help and I'm holding you to it."

Four

He squirmed uneasily in his chair. Now that he knew just what she was looking for, he was a little warier than usual. There wasn't a chance in hell he was going to get involved with a virgin looking to explore sex. Down that road lay—well, all kinds of things he wasn't interested in.

"Exactly what kind of 'help' are we talking about here?" Mike asked, determinedly keeping his gaze locked with hers. Despite the fact that her blue eyes looked soft and tempting, it was still safer than letting his gaze drift over that body she'd managed to hide until tonight.

Nora laughed, the sound rising up, filling the quiet room and settling over him like a promise.

"Jeez, relax, Mike." She lifted her cup and took a long sip of the fragrant coffee. "You look like a man who's just been stood up against a wall, given a blindfold and asked for his last words."

"No, I don't." He was better at hiding his emotions than *that,* wasn't he?

"Right." Nora shook her head, and he refused to notice how many different colors of blond her hair really was. Besides, she was talking. Again.

"It's not like I want *you* to do the deed personally."

In fact, she sounded pretty damn appalled at the notion. "Well," he said, pretty sure he'd just been insulted. "That's good."

Nora got up, walked to the cookie jar and filled a plate with a dozen or so of her fresh baked cookies. Carrying them back to the table, she set them down in front of him, took one for herself and sat down again.

Mike glanced at the plate. Chocolate chip, peanut butter, cinnamon sugar. If he *was* looking for a wife...which he wasn't...he'd still avoid Nora. Being married to a woman who could bake like this could put five hundred pounds on a guy.

"I mean, everyone in town knows that you're not interested in women."

He froze, startled. "Excuse me?"

She laughed again. "Sorry. That came out wrong. I just meant that you're not interested in commitment. I mean, ever since Vicky left, you've practically had Stay Away tattooed on your forehead."

Everything inside him went cold and still. It took every ounce of his self-control not to crumble the cookie he held into a pile of crumbs. He wasn't going to get drawn into a discussion about his ex-wife. Not with anyone. And apparently, Nora could see that fact in his expression as well.

"Oops." She covered a flash of embarrassment by taking another gulp of coffee. Then cradling the cup in her hands, she lifted her gaze to his and, wincing, said, "Sorry about that."

"No problem."

"Yeah, so I see. Look, I didn't mean to mention the *V* word."

Mike willed his hands to relax. Willed his muscles to unclench. Willed his apparently clear-as-glass expression to shift into one of complete ambivalence. "I told you. No problem. Vicky's in the past."

Mike was the first to admit that since Vicky packed up, picked up and left two years ago, he hadn't exactly been a social animal. He preferred life on the ranch. There, all he had to deal with were the animals, the price of oranges and frost. And of course, Emily. His brain fuzzed out a little as he thought of his daughter.

Five years old and the one good thing he and Vicky had managed to do together.

He could understand how a woman could get fed up with marriage, with ranch life…hell, with *him*. What he'd never be able to comprehend is how a woman could walk away from her own daughter without a backward glance. But then Vicky had never wanted to be a mother, had she? And when she left, she'd told him flat out that he could have sole custody.

Which worked out fine as far as Mike was concerned. One day, he'd have to find a way to explain to Emily just why her mother had chosen to abandon her. But until then, the two of them were a team and he'd protect that child with everything he had. And if that meant steering clear of women until his daughter was eighteen, then that was a small price to pay. He didn't want a string of women going in and out of Emily's life. He wanted her to have stability. Security. But most of all, he didn't want her heart broken because she'd become attached to daddy's girlfriend only to have that woman disappear from their world.

Nope. And if that made him a hermit, then he'd just have to live with it.

Still, just because he wasn't looking for a relationship, that didn't make him *dead*.

"Uh-huh. If she's in the past, why does just the mention of her name freeze you over?" She looked at him for a long, slow minute. He could almost feel the seconds ticking past as he stared into those blue eyes of hers. A part of his mind wondered why he'd never noticed before just how many shades of blue were centered in her gaze.

Focus, he told himself again.

"I just don't like to be reminded, that's all."

She turned her coffee cup idly. "Emily's a fairly big reminder, don't you think?"

"That's different. Emily is...*Emily.*"

Nora nodded slowly. "She's a sweetheart."

He relaxed a little. "Yeah, she is."

One second ticked past, then two, then three, while they stared at each other across the kitchen table. With the darkness crouched just beyond the window, and the silence hovering in the room, they sat together in the warm, cozy kitchen and it felt...*intimate,* somehow.

"Anyway," Nora said, a bit louder than necessary as she forced the word *intimate* out of her brain, "back on target. The point is, you're not looking for a wife, so you're safe."

One corner of his mouth tipped up. "Just what every man wants to hear."

"At least you can relax knowing you're out of the running."

"But every other man in town is fair game?"

"Hey, a girl's gotta plan ahead," Nora said, ignoring the decidedly insulted tone of his voice. "This is not only about losing my virginity—it's about finding Mr. Right.''

''In Tesoro?''

She frowned to herself. ''True, the options are a little limited, but I'm sure I can make this work. I know the men here. I don't know anyone in the city. And I'm not the kind of woman who can stroll into a bar and pick up a stranger. That would just be too…icky.'' She sighed and picked up her coffee cup again. ''Besides, my mother's been reading the singles ads and assures me that there are *lots* of nice men in Monterey.''

''Singles ads? You?''

He sounded so genuinely surprised by that notion, Nora felt a bit better. ''Thanks for that,'' she said, flashing him a quick smile. ''But my mother's more eager to find me a man than I am. The woman's just dying for more grandchildren.''

''You have sisters,'' he pointed out.

''Yeah, but Frannie and Jenny have done their part already. I'm the last holdout.'' Disgusted, she leaned back in her chair, folded her arms beneath her breasts and propped her bare feet up on the chair closest to her. ''I swear, this whole 'virtue thing' has gotten way out of hand. It's become a liability instead of an asset.''

''You could just keep the whole 'virgin thing' a secret.''

"Thought about that," she admitted, shaking her head again. "But it's no good. I think guys have radar about this sort of thing. They home right in on a virgin and then steer a wide path around her." She shot him a knowing look.

"Point taken."

"So, since you owe me one, for breaking up my little plan..."

"Some plan—"

"And—" she raised her voice to talk over him "—since you personally are out of the running, I think it's only fair that you help me find 'the guy.'"

"Now I'm a matchmaker?"

"More of a trapper."

"I think this is against the rules for a member of the male gender."

She smiled again and he felt the warmth of it slap into him.

"I won't tell if you don't."

"Trust me," he vowed. "I'm not telling."

"Good. Then, between the two of us, we should be able to find the right guy."

How this had happened, Mike had no idea. All he'd done was try to do the right thing. Help her out of a bad situation. And now he was stuck in a situation that made her little scene with Bill Hammond look like a picnic.

"Then it's a deal?" She held out one hand across the table.

He thought about making one last stab at getting out of this. But then he looked into those eyes of hers again and he knew it was a lost cause. Mike took her hand in his, ignored that soul-searing flash of warmth and muttered "Deal" before quickly releasing her again.

But the warmth stayed with him and Mike had the distinct feeling that he was going to regret this deal for a long, long time.

"So, what happened with Bill?"

It was late afternoon the day after the reception and business was pretty slow. Nora had had only one or two customers since noon, so she took a seat behind the counter, balanced the phone receiver on her shoulder and answered Molly's question. "Nothing. Absolutely nothing."

There was a long, thoughtful silence before her best friend said, "But you left with him. And you never came back."

"Yeah, well," Nora said, checking off a list of grocery supplies as she talked, "there was a slight hitch in the plan."

"What kind of hitch?"

"Mike showed up out of nowhere and sent Bill into the bushes."

"Mike Fallon?"

"The one and only."

"Oooh. Now this is getting interesting."

"Not really." Although sitting with Mike at her kitchen table last night had been…nice. In the last few years, they'd hardly talked at all, except for the few words they exchanged over her counter. And maybe it was the margaritas talking, but he'd seemed so… different last night. More approachable. More… lustable. Jeez. Was that even a word?

"Oh, come on, let an old married woman enjoy her fantasies, will ya? Gorgeous Mike Fallon, riding to the rescue—he did ride to the rescue, right?"

"Oh, yeah. I'm guessing Bill's not real fond of him today."

"Well good. I mean, Bill Hammond isn't exactly the stuff dreams are made of."

"I know, but—"

"No buts. You deserve better, Nor."

True. Not that Bill was a troll or anything, but for heaven's sake. Did she really want to give up her long-held virginity to a man who wouldn't even notice? Funny how your ideas could change in one evening. Just yesterday, she'd been ready to do almost anything to leave chastity behind. Today, she wanted a little…more.

Behind her, the bell attached to the front door jangled out a welcome and announced a customer's arrival.

"Someone's here," she told Molly. "Gotta go."

"Okay, but I demand up-to-the-minute reports."

"Promise," Nora said, and hung up the phone smiling. Standing up, she turned around to greet...an empty store. Frowning, she moved around the counter, and as soon as she did, she spotted her customer.

"Well, hi," she said. "I didn't see you."

Emily Fallon smiled at her and Nora's heart melted. "That's 'cuz I'm still really little."

"I guess you are," Nora said, nodding. "So what can I do for you today, Miss Fallon?"

The little girl giggled and held out her closed right fist. When she opened it, she revealed a crumpled-up one dollar bill. "Daddy says I can have two cookies."

"He did, did he?" Nora said thoughtfully, and let her gaze slide past the child to the wide front windows and the street beyond. Mike stood just outside, and for a second, Nora noticed her heartbeat quicken. Which was weird. After all, she'd known Mike for years, and until last night, she'd never thought of him as more than Emily's dad and a pretty nice guy.

Suddenly, though, those long legs of his looked delectable in his worn jeans. His scuffed boots, crossed at the ankle, looked...sexy. The worn, long-sleeved blue shirt he wore only made his already-broad chest look wider, more muscular. And his green eyes as he watched her through the window seemed deeper, more mysterious, than she remembered.

Her stomach pitched suddenly and Nora pulled in a long, steadying breath in a futile attempt to get a grip on her wildly raging hormones.

This is ridiculous, she told herself. Mike wasn't interested in her. Or anyone. He wasn't going to be the man to help her through her "problem." So there was absolutely no point in indulging in what could probably be staggeringly wonderful fantasies.

"Miss Nora..."

She shook her head, but didn't manage to dislodge any of said fantasies. Determined, though, she looked back at his daughter. Good. Focus there. On a sweet face, with freckles dotting a tiny nose. On a pair of lopsided pigtails and a wide grin that displayed one dimpled cheek. On green eyes that were so like her father's...

Cut it out, Nora.

"Two cookies. Chocolate chip, right?" she asked unnecessarily as she walked behind the counter and filled the order. Like every other child Nora had ever known, Emily had particular likes and dislikes, with chocolate chip cookies being high on the approved list.

"Yes'm."

She smiled to herself at the polite and grownup-sounding child, then walked back to Emily and handed her a small white bag. "Here you go, honey."

"Thank you."

"Shall we see if your daddy wants a cookie, too?"

Emily laughed. "Oh, he doesn't. I heard him tell Rick he wasn't gonna eat sugar anymore."

"Is that right?" Nora looked from the girl to the man still standing safely outside the bakery. Telling his foreman that he was swearing off sugar, was he? And apparently he figured if he didn't actually step inside the bakery, he'd be safely out of reach. Did he really think she'd let him off the hook that easily?

"Let's go talk to your daddy and see if we can't change his mind." Nora took Emily's small hand in hers and kept hold of it while she pushed through the door and stepped onto the sidewalk.

Mike straightened up instantly, coming out of the lazy lean against a light pole like a man ready to bolt. Late-afternoon sunshine spilled down on the street from a cloudless blue sky, and all around them, the town was bustling.

"Hi, Nora."

"Mike."

"Miss Nora says you should have a cookie." Emily looked from one adult to the other, her pigtails swinging as she turned her head from side to side.

"Swearing off sugar, huh?"

Mike scowled. "Just cutting back."

"Sugar in general, or just my bakery?"

"Nora," he said, "I just figured that after you slept

it off—'' He broke off, glanced at his daughter and reworded that. ''After a good night's sleep, you'd see that this whole idea is crazy and want to forget about it.''

''You figured wrong.''

''Apparently.''

''So,'' Nora said, gently running one hand across the top of Emily's head, ''I was thinking I'd come out to the ranch tonight and we could make some plans.''

He squinted into the sunlight, scraped one hand across his jaw and said, ''You're not going to let go of this at all, are you?''

''Not a chance,'' she said.

He sighed heavily and said, ''Fine. Tonight.''

''Are you gonna come over and bring cookies, Miss Nora?''

Nora looked down at the little girl and smiled. ''How about I come over early and you and I can make cookies together?''

''Oh, you don't have to—'' he started to say.

''Goody,'' Emily crowed, her small voice undermining her father's protest.

''Terrific,'' Nora said, lifting her gaze to meet Mike's. ''Then I'll see you in an hour or two, okay?''

He just stared at her for a long minute before caving. ''I'm outmanned and outgunned. Guess we'll see you at the ranch in a while.''

''Can't wait,'' she assured him.

As Mike took his daughter's hand and headed toward their car, he felt Nora's gaze on him as surely as he would have her touch. With Emily's chatter rattling around him, he tried to tell himself that having Nora in his house would be no big deal.

But his heartbeat quickened at the thought and his body felt suddenly tight and uncomfortable. He figured his hormones were fighting it out with his brain.

He just didn't know which was going to win.

Five

"An' can we make some with little candies on 'em?"

"You bet we can," Nora said, and wiped a splotch of flour off the tip of Emily's nose.

"This is fun, Nora," the little girl said, and slapped her small hands down onto the dough. "Daddy doesn't let me cook 'cuz I'm too small."

Oops. Nora inwardly cringed a bit. Maybe she should have checked this out with Mike first. On the other hand, he wasn't here and she was. So, as long as they weren't cooking over an open fire on the linoleum, she didn't really see a problem. Although, she thought, glancing down at the worn, faux-brick floor-ing…maybe an open fire wouldn't be such a bad idea.

"Well, we'll just have to tell him what a good job you did, won't we?"

Emily gave her a grin filled with absolute delight, and Nora figured that reward would be worth any has-sle she had to face later with Mike.

And speaking of Mike, where the heck was he, any-way? Nora had already been at the ranch for two hours and there was still no sign of him. Donna Dixon, the ranch foreman's wife, had been here watching Emily when Nora arrived. At eight months pregnant, the woman had been only too happy to turn Emily's care over to Nora so she could go home and lie down.

Left to their own devices, Nora and Emily had played two games, colored pictures and then had tea with her favorite dolls. When tea time was over, the child took Nora on a tour of the house, and Nora was surprised to note that except for Emily's room, which was every little girl's fantasy bedroom, the ranch house was very plainly decorated.

For Emily, there were soft blue walls, a canopy bed, lace and ruffles, bookcases stuffed with the classics along with dozens of nighttime storybooks. Not to mention enough dolls and stuffed animals to populate Santa's workshop. But the rest of the house was sim-ply furnished, with no little touches that added warmth. The great room held a couple of comfortable-looking sofas and one worn chair facing a huge open hearth. The minute she saw it, Nora's brain started whirling with ideas to cozy up the big space. She'd like to be turned loose on the house with a few gallons of paint and a little imagination.

But it was the kitchen that really called to her. It was a terrific room, with all kinds of potential. But the beige walls and plain pine cabinets practically screamed for attention. In her mind's eye, she saw what it could look like and her mouth nearly watered with her itch to do something about it. Still, it wasn't her business, was it? Mike hadn't invited her in to redecorate his house. Heck, he hadn't *invited* her at all. She'd practically forced herself on him.

"Are the cookies done yet?"

"Hmm?" Nora dragged her mind back to the present and looked at Emily. "Oh. Cookies. Let's check, okay?"

The little girl hopped down from her stool and hurried to the oven door.

"Don't touch it now, it's hot."

Emily practically danced in place, but she slapped her tiny hands together and held on tight, as if to keep from reaching for the cookies.

Grinning, Nora picked up a hot pad, opened the oven door and was instantly greeted by a wave of heat and the glorious scent of hot chocolate chips. "Done," she pronounced, and pulled the tray out. In a few seconds, she had the cookies scooped up and onto a cooling tray, the next batch loaded and the oven door shut again.

Emily breathed deep and then looked at Nora. "Can we have one?"

Any reasonable adult would no doubt say, *Of course not. You have to wait until after dinner so you won't spoil your appetite.* Nora's own mother was a big believer in the "no snack" theory. But Nora wasn't about to look into those shining green eyes and say no.

"Sure we can," she said instead. "Nothing better than gooey, warm cookies."

Emily sucked in a gulp of air and held it while Nora picked up the tray and held it out to the little girl. "They're hot, so be careful."

"I will." She plucked a nice fat one from the rack and waited until Nora picked one for herself, then set the rack back on the counter before biting into it. Grinning, she mumbled, "S'good."

"It sure is," Nora said, smiling at the smear of chocolate on the child's mouth and the glint of pride in her eyes. Poor little thing. No mom to share these little adventures with. And a father, who though loving, was obviously a late worker. True, Emily did have Donna during the day, but since the foreman's wife was really centered on her own coming child, she didn't have the attention to give Emily. Nora felt a small twinge in her heart as she smiled and said softly, "You're a good baker."

"I am, huh?" The girl wiped her free hand on the apron that was tied around her chest and hung almost to her feet. "I can tell Daddy I'm a good cook, can't I?"

"I'm sure he'll be very impressed," Nora assured her, and made a mental note to make sure Mike was suitably proud of Emily's accomplishment.

"Can we make some more?"

Nora laughed and stood up, brushing one hand across the girl's forehead, lifting straw-colored bangs that felt like silk. "Let's finish these first, okay?"

"'Kay," Emily agreed, and climbed the stool again to take her place beside the oak cooking island. Carefully, just as Nora had shown her, the little girl scooped out spoonful after spoonful of cookie dough and gently dropped them onto another cookie sheet.

Nora kept one eye on the child and one eye on the kitchen window. Outside, twilight deepened. Across the ranch yard, she could see lamplight glinting in Rick and Donna's windows. She was used to looking out her own windows and seeing streetlamps and cars passing along the road. Here, on the edges of town, darkness was more complete. More...*dark*. Walking across the kitchen, she opened the back door and let the cool evening breeze drift past her.

Except for the sound of Emily singing to herself

under her breath, the silence was awesome. Nora
would have thought this much quiet would be unnerv-
ing. Instead she found it…soothing. There was a sense
of peacefulness about the whole place, the silent house
and the wide openness surrounding it that seemed almost magical.

She glanced at her watch.

And wondered again where Mike was and just how
long he was going to stall before coming home.

Mike stayed out on the ranch until it was too damn
dark to get anything else done. Rick, his foreman, had
called it a day more than an hour ago, heading back
to the small house on the ranch that he shared with
his pregnant wife. But then Rick was eager to get
home. He didn't have a woman on a mission waiting
for him.

The first few stars winked into existence and glit-
tered against a deep purple sky. He pulled off his hat,
raked his fingers through his hair and told himself that
he had to go home sometime. It wasn't just Nora sitting in his house waiting. Emily would be wondering
where he was pretty soon.

He climbed into the truck, slammed the door and
fired up the engine. He'd stalled as long as he could.
If he stayed out here much later, he'd need a sleeping
bag. Besides, why should he let Nora keep him away
from his own house? Throwing the truck into gear, he

flicked on the headlights and headed toward home. The ruts in the road rattled the truck and shook the rocks in Mike's head.

"Idiot," he muttered, and braced his left arm on the window ledge. "It's just Nora Bailey. You've seen her at least a couple of times a week for years. Now all of a sudden you can't be in the same room with her?"

He slapped his hand against the steering wheel and made a sharp right into the drive leading to the house. Gravel crunched beneath the tires and ground out a familiar welcome. As he shut off the engine and climbed out of the truck, he told himself again that there was no reason to be wary of Nora. She'd made it plain enough that he wasn't in the running for the task she needed done. And that was just fine with him. So fine. He snatched his hat off, crumpled the brim in one tight fist and stopped dead outside the kitchen window.

Inside, two blond heads were bent together. Nora and Emily, side by side at the cooking island, were laughing together and making cookies. At that moment, Mike's daughter lifted her head, looked into Nora's eyes and damn near *beamed*. Her little face was lit from within. Delight sparkled in her eyes and the dimple in her cheek had never looked deeper. There was only one word to describe the expression on his little girl's face. *Adoration*. Clearly, she'd found her hero in Nora.

But before he could wonder if that was a good thing or a bad thing, Emily spotted him and whooped out a welcome. She clambered off the kitchen stool and he headed for the door. His long legs couldn't carry him as fast as an excited little girl could move. In seconds, she had the door open and was jumping at him, arms wide.

Mike scooped her up, swung her around in a tight circle, then propped his forearm beneath her bottom to support her as she clung to him like a burr. Her small arms wrapped around his neck and hugged tight. And just as it did every night, Mike's heart melted. He held his whole world in his arms, and he never forgot to thank whatever gods had sent this child. She was everything to him.

"Daddy, I *cooked!*" She pulled her head back to look at him and gave him a smile that always turned him into a soft lump of clay that Emily could push and shove around any way she wanted to.

"You did, huh?"

She nodded so fiercely that her pigtails swung wildly around her head. "I made cookies." Emily turned her head to look at the woman just stepping around the oak island. "Nora helped, but I did it and everything."

Before he could speak, Nora's voice cut across his child's high-pitched words.

"Emily told me that she's not allowed to cook, but

I thought that just this once wouldn't be so bad and that you'd understand and—''

Mike held up one hand to cut the stream of conversation off. It sounded as though she was warning him not to be mad. As though she thought he might come down on Emily for a decision an adult made. Did she really think he was that big a jerk? Besides, even if he'd wanted to, he wouldn't have been able to maintain anger while looking into Emily's happy face. She was just so proud of her accomplishment.

''Do you want one, Daddy?''

He tore his gaze from Nora to look into the eyes so much like his own. ''Absolutely.'' Mike lifted her off his hip, set her on her feet and gave her backside a pat. ''Go pick me a good one, okay?''

''I'll get you the best one of all,'' she promised, and practically skipped over to the cooling rack.

While Emily was busy, Nora sidled up to him. ''Thanks for not spoiling her good time by being mad.''

''I'm not an ogre, y'know.''

''Never said you were,'' she countered. ''But Emily told me you don't want her cooking and—''

He hung his hat on the rack just inside the door, then shoved both hands into his jeans pockets before saying, ''That's because Donna's not much of a cook. Almost burned down the kitchen once when she forgot and left a pan on the stove.''

"Yikes."

"Exactly."

"Okay then, so you won't mind if Emily and I do a little baking from time to time?"

From time to time? So then this wasn't a one-time-only visit? He looked at her through narrowed eyes. "You figuring on being here a lot, are you?"

"Well, at least until we solve my problem," she said, half turning to keep an eye on Emily, who was examining each and every cookie. "How long do you figure that'll take?"

How long to find a man worthy of Nora Bailey?

He was just beginning to suspect that it might be an impossible task.

Then Emily was back, carrying two cookies. She handed one each to the adults. "Taste it, Daddy."

Nora lifted hers and took a small, dainty bite of the chocolate chip cookie. He watched her mouth and felt tortured as she licked warm chocolate off her bottom lip with a long, slow sweep of her tongue.

"Aren't you hungry, Daddy?" Emily demanded.

"I sure am," he said tightly. But not for cookies. Nora gave him a knowing look and a quick smile, then turned and walked across the kitchen. His gaze dropped to the sway of her behind, and he wondered if jeans that tight shouldn't be illegal.

To distract himself, he shoved the cookie in his mouth and chewed with a vengeance. Emily was delighted. But Mike was still hungry—and there weren't enough chocolate chips in the country to ease the ache building inside him.

For the next couple of weeks, Nora spent nearly as much time at the ranch as she did at the bakery. She was still up before dawn to do the baking, but nearly every day she left the bakery in the early afternoon to make the drive out to the Fallon ranch. And, each time she did, she caught herself closing just a bit earlier than the last time. Heck, if this kept up, she'd soon be serving the breakfast crowd, then shutting down for the day.

But she couldn't seem to help herself. Sure, it had all started with the idea of Mike helping her find a man. But it was developing into so much more than that. She really looked forward to spending time with Emily. The little girl touched corners of Nora's heart she hadn't even known were lonely. The child was so hungry for a mother's love and attention that she soaked up whatever affection Nora gave her and then handed it back ten times over.

Mike, though, was a different story. Nora leaned her forearms on the tall, whitewashed rail fence surrounding a paddock. In the center of the wide ring, Mike stood, holding a long leather leash in one hand. On the other end of the leash, a beautiful horse cantered around the edges of the circle, tossing its head as if trying to shake him.

But Mike kept up a steady stream of soothing words as he worked the animal. Most of it was nonsense, but the rhythm of his speech and the deep rumble of his voice combined to nearly hypnotize the horse…and Nora. Her gaze locked on him, she followed him as he turned in a slow circle. His faded blue work shirt was worn and sweat-stained. His jeans were covered in dirt and grime. His boots were filthy, and the hat he wore was tilted low over his eyes, shading them to the point where she couldn't even see them. But, then, she didn't have to. She knew only too well the power of that direct stare.

Hadn't she been dreaming about those eyes of his for nearly a week? Her mouth went dry and her stomach swirled with nerves and anticipation, and with something tight and dark and hot that made every cell in her body sit up and weep for mercy.

It was torture, pure and simple. But it was also a torture she willingly put herself through every afternoon. It had become a routine. Something she looked forward to. Spending this time with Mike, watching him work the animals with a sure and steady hand was—okay, exciting.

She shifted her gaze to take in the ranch yard and the wide-open spaces beyond. It was just so beautiful out here. She couldn't imagine being able to wake up every morning and have this be the first thing you saw. Being away from town felt energizing. The lack of people and noise gave her the chance to think. And the slower pace gave way to time for daydreams.

And that thought brought her right back to Mike. Her favorite daydream.

"Okay, that's enough for today," Mike called out, and Nora blinked, dismissing those late-night fantasies as the product of a *way*-overworked imagination. She willed her nerves into submission and watched as Mike tossed the leather leash to Rick, then turn and headed toward her.

"Pretty horse," she said when she was sure her voice would work.

"Stubborn, too," Mike pointed out, and, grinning, tugged leather gloves off his hands. "It's going to take me forever to convince that mare to wear a saddle and bridle."

He sounded disgusted, but Nora wasn't fooled. She'd noted the gleam of admiration in his eyes as he watched the horse being led back to the stable. Chuckling, she said, "You love it."

Mike glanced at her, almost surprised. "Yeah. Guess I do." Pulling his hat off, he ran one hand through his hair, then leaned an elbow on the top rung of the fence. "Boarding and training horses are the fun part of living on the ranch."

"And what's the part you don't love?"

His gaze locked with hers. "Not a damn thing. I like being out here. I like everything about living on the ranch. I don't plan on moving to a town. *Ever.*"

Nora had the distinct impression that there was a message in that last statement. But since she hadn't a clue what that might be, she took what he'd said at face value. "I don't blame you."

"Huh?"

She glanced at him, then turned her face into the wind and stared out beyond the paddock and the ranch yard. Off in the distance, the orchards spread out in neat, orderly rows like soldiers lined up for inspection. Overhead, the sky was a deep, vivid blue, with a handful of marshmallow clouds scuttling across its surface.

"I said I don't blame you," she repeated. "It's beautiful here. And so quiet."

"Yeah."

"I mean," she went on, "I know Tesoro's a small town, but still, sometimes the noise and all the people get to me."

"Uh-huh."

Reacting to the tone of his voice, she turned her head to look at him. "You don't believe me."

"Let's just say, I've heard that one before."

"Is that right?" she asked. "From who?"

"Vicky." He bit off the word and his mouth looked as if he'd tasted something bitter.

Nora's stomach jittered and she told herself she

should let it go. Heck, the look in his eyes told her he
clearly didn't want to talk about it. But there was
something else there, too. Some echo of disappointment. Some lasting shred of hurt that tugged at her
and wouldn't allow her to keep quiet.

"What didn't she like?"

He inhaled slowly, deeply, and shifted his gaze from
hers to stare out over the ranch. "Asking me what she
did like would take less time."

"Okay," she said. "Consider it asked."

Slowly, he turned his head until he was looking at
her again. "Nothing. Not the quiet, not the solitude,
not Emily—and at the end, not me, either."

"She was an idiot."

He shrugged, but Nora wasn't fooled. Old pain was
still too close to the surface here. "So was I," he said.
"I thought desire was a good start for a marriage."
He turned his gaze directly on her and Nora read regret
shining clearly in those dark green depths. "I let my
hormones guide me once. I won't do it again."

"Nobody's asking you to," she reminded him.
Though that wasn't really accurate. Since her own hormones were singing, she wouldn't mind a bit if his
did a quick dance or two.

"You seem to like it out here," he said, and the
abrupt change of subject startled her for an instant.

But she went with it and saw relief crowd his features. "I do. It's gorgeous. And the ranch house is so

big. The whole place feels big, though. Wide open—you know, 'where the buffalo roam' kind of feel."

He laughed shortly and Nora relished the deep rumble of sound. "No buffalo. Just horses, a few orchards—"

"It's enough," she interrupted him, and let her gaze wander briefly again before looking back at him. "It's a great place to raise kids."

Oops. There went that thundercloud chasing across his face again.

"That was the plan," he admitted. "But things don't always work out like you think they will."

His voice had dropped so low that she barely heard the last few words he uttered. It must have cost him to talk about his ex-wife. A part of Nora wanted to go find Vicky and give her a good, swift kick. But since she couldn't very well do that, she settled for changing the subject one more time. The instant she did, she saw relief flood his eyes.

"Well, you'll just have to do a better job of finding me a man than you did in finding yourself a wife."

"Shouldn't be tough," he muttered.

"Good." Resting her chin on her forearms, she looked at him through wide, innocent eyes. "I've been thinking. What about Tony Diaz?"

He pulled his head back and looked at her as though her hair was on fire. "Are you nuts? He's twenty years older than you."

Nora hid an inward smile and congratulated herself on obviously striking a nerve. "Experienced."

"Old."

"Then he'd probably consider me a sweet young thing," she pointed out, thoroughly enjoying herself now. "That's a definite plus."

"You're twenty-eight. Not exactly ready for medicare."

"Hey, age is in the eye of the beholder."

"Tony sells shoes at a department store."

Okay, this wasn't really fair. Nora was getting way too big a kick out of teasing him. She was no more interested in Tony Diaz than she was in dancing naked down Main Street. "A steady job," she said. "People with feet will always need shoes."

"And the fact that he has a daughter the same age as you?"

"We can raid each other's closets."

Mike stared at her for a long minute, until he finally noticed the gleam in her eyes and then he bit back the laugh crawling up his throat. "You're pulling my chain."

Blond eyebrows lifted and one corner of her mouth twitched. "Not yet. Would you like me to?"

Six

He was pretty sure his heart stopped for a second. Images filled his brain, racing through his mind at top speed. He had a feeling she knew it, too. She chewed at her bottom lip and, with every tug, he felt a like tug somewhere deep inside him.

Mike shifted uncomfortably, scowled a bit and refused to take the bait. Instead, he asked, a bit harsher than he'd planned to, "Why are you here?"

The slight smile on her face faded slowly. "Do you mean existentially speaking or literally, *here?*"

"Literally, thanks," he ground out.

"Our bargain," she reminded him.

The damn bargain. Talk about making deals with the devil. He hadn't had a minute's peace since agreeing to this whole thing. "You know, that's not really working out so well."

"Only because every man I suggest, you shoot down."

True. Damn it. *He'd* noticed that, but he'd been sort of hoping she hadn't. It's not that he didn't want to help her find some guy—or maybe it was. He couldn't be sure anymore. All he knew was that whenever she suggested one of the men in town, he had a ready reason why she should stay the hell away from the guy.

Too old.

Too young.

Too fat.

Too poor.

Drank too much.

Hell, it was ridiculous. Most of the men they'd talked about had been Mike's friends for years. He'd never had a problem with any of them. Until it came time to set Nora up with one of them.

For some reason or other, he just didn't like the idea of her being with…*hell, admit it. Anyone.* Which made for a big problem. Because he wasn't going to be sucked into trouble by his hormones again.

When he'd first met Vicky, his body had gone on high alert and all he could think about was having her.

Then, once he *had* her, everything had gone straight down the tubes. There was no way he was going to let his body do the thinking for him again.

So why the heck didn't he find Nora a nice guy and get her out of his hair? His mind? His dreams?

Pushing away from the fence, he took a step or two farther, as if that extra foot of space between them would make all the difference. Then he looked at her again. "You're right."

"I am?"

"Absolutely."

"You have no idea just how much a woman loves hearing a man say that," she said, "but in the interest of clarity, I'm right about *what,* exactly?"

"About me shooting down your suggestions."

She nodded sagely. "Ah. So you're in favor of Tony, then?"

He snapped her a quick look. "No. He *is* too old for you. God, Nora, you're looking for a man. Not a father figure."

"Okay," she said, with a little shrug that caused the rounded neckline of her T-shirt to slide off her left shoulder. Mike's gaze locked on that patch of creamy skin and he wondered if it felt as smooth as it looked. He fisted his hands to keep from reaching for her to find out. "So who'd you have in mind?"

He racked his brain, trying to come up with somebody he hadn't already dismissed. And just when he figured he was going to come up dry, a name occurred to him. "Seth," he blurted, grateful for the inspiration. "Seth Thomas."

Nora frowned thoughtfully. "The deputy?"

"Why not?" Mike countered, forcing himself to push the idea. "He's new in town. Probably doesn't know too many people yet."

She looked at him, and for one long moment, he lost himself in those blue eyes of hers. But then he remembered that Nora wasn't for him. He reminded himself that the last two weeks didn't mean squat. She'd been coming out here to have him help her find someone *else.* The fact that he'd gotten used to having her around meant nothing. The fact that she and Emily had become the best of friends—well, that did worry him. Sooner or later, Nora would stop hanging around out here so much—and for the sake of his sanity, it had better be sooner—and then Emily would be hurt, missing her friend.

But just think, he told himself, how much worse she'd be hurt if she thought she had a shot at getting a brand-new mother only to be let down.

Nope. Better this way. Better for everyone. Especially for Seth Thomas, the lucky bastard.

"You know what?" Nora said after a long minute or two of strained silence. "You're right. Seth is new in town. Who better for me to try my 'wiles' on?"

She stepped back from the fence, an unreadable expression on her face. But all Mike could see were her eyes. Eyes that suddenly looked huge and innocent and...*disappointed?*

"Nora..." Mike started, but a second later he was interrupted, and it was just as well, since he didn't know what the hell he'd been about to say.

"Nora!" Emily's high, thin voice floated out of the house, and a half second later, the girl herself came sprinting into the yard.

Nora broke eye contact with Mike and turned to look at the little girl eagerly racing toward her. "What is it, sweetie?"

"I finished my picture," Emily called out, nearly breathless with excitement. She skidded to a stop beside Nora, grabbed her hand and started tugging the woman toward the house. "You hafta see. I made it for you. Special."

"Well, I can't wait to see it, then," Nora told her, and scooped the child up to prop her on one hip. Gently, she smoothed the child's flyaway blond hair back from her face. Then, without looking back at him, Nora lifted one hand in a salute. "See you around, Mike. This is girl stuff."

"Yeah, Daddy," Emily repeated with a smile, watching him from over Nora's shoulder. "Girl stuff."

He took a step after them, then stopped himself. His gaze locked on the two of them, and for a second he felt like the outsider here. Nora and his daughter had somehow become a "team" in the last couple of weeks. They were drawing a circle of warmth around each other and it was all Mike could do to keep from stepping into the center of it.

And before he could forget all of his hard-won lessons, he turned his back on the house and walked, alone, to the cold, dark barn.

The bakery was busy.

Both of Nora's part-time employees were racing around, filling orders, pouring coffee and making change. Outside, morning sunlight lit up Main Street like a spotlight. On the sidewalks, people were hustling through their shopping chores and stopping to chat with old friends.

But, at Nora's, there was no time for chatting. And she was grateful. As long as she kept busy, she didn't have to think about last night.

Stupid, she told herself, and sliced up another steaming pan of lemon rolls. She made quick, deft cuts, moving on instinct, as her brain rattled noisily in her head.

"Pulling my chain?"

"Not yet. Want me to?"

Oh, God. She'd made an idiot of herself.

Why in heaven's name was she even *trying* to flirt with Mike? She wasn't supposed to be developing "feelings" for Mike Fallon. He was just the means to an end. Her little helper. An elf in Santa's workshop, for goodness' sake.

She stopped slicing for a second and in that blink of time saw again Mike's reaction to her teasing. If she'd been blind, she would still have seen the Go Away sign in his eyes. And what had she done? Kept talking, that's what. Tell him he had lousy taste in wives. "Good going, Nora. That was thoughtful."

Grumbling, she finished slicing the lemon rolls, set the knife down and reached for a spatula. "You're an idiot, Nora," she muttered, then shifted to one side and used the spatula to scoop up the rolls and set them on a paper-doily-covered platter.

"Terry," she called. When a short teenager with freckles poked her head around the door, she said, "Here're the rolls."

"Good," the girl said, stepping into the room to take the tray. "The natives are getting restless."

"Ooh," Molly said as she, too, stepped into the kitchen, "then I'd better grab one of those before the slavering hordes get them all." She plucked a lemon roll off the top of the plate and grinned as Terry disappeared back into the main room.

"Hi," Nora said, then looked for the stroller Molly usually had with her. "Where's the baby?"

"With Donna Dixon, out front. She wanted to see the baby and I wanted to see you." Licking icing off her fingers, Molly walked across the kitchen, leaned one hip on the counter and stared at her best friend. "So, Jeff tells me that you've got a date with the new deputy tonight."

Nora dusted her hands with flour, then plunged both fists into a mound of dough that had been set aside to rise. Kneading always worked out her tensions and today she needed the outlet more than usual. Seth Thomas. The guy Mike had thrown at her like a bone tossed to a guard dog to distract the animal long enough so you could escape. Ah, yes. So romantic.

"News travels fast."

"Could have been faster," Molly pointed out, then took a bite of lemon roll. "I mean, I would have thought my very best friend would tell me herself when she's got a hot date. But noooo…I have to hear it from my husband."

"Jeff's got a big mouth."

"Yeah, I know. One of the reasons I love him. Can't keep a secret, so I find out everything." She walked around the kitchen island, grabbed a coffee mug and poured herself a cup. "Except, of course, why said best friend didn't call me."

Nora winced. True. She'd been letting a lot of things slide the last couple of weeks. Her business. Her friends. Her family. All to spend time with a man who so clearly wasn't interested in her. *Idiot.* "Sorry," she said lamely. "I meant to call, but I've been busy and—"

"Yeah," Molly interrupted around another bite of lemon roll, "busy hanging out at Mike Fallon's place."

"There's that news bulletin again," Nora muttered. Honestly, it was impossible to keep things quiet in Tesoro. Everyone knew everyone else's business and felt justified in spreading that knowledge everywhere they went. But then, she'd been spending so much time at Mike's place, it was a wonder her mother hadn't had wedding invitations printed up.

"Just what's been going on out there, anyway?" Molly asked. Then she gasped as an idea struck and she nearly choked on a piece of pastry. After the resulting coughing fit ended, she asked breathlessly, "You didn't—you haven't—not with Mike Fallon?"

"*No.*" Nora's denial was flat and too disgusted to be taken for a lie. "I'm still in the ranks of the 'virgins-this-old-should-be-shot category.'"

"Oh." She took a sip of coffee. "Well, that's disappointing."

Nora stopped kneading, pulled one fist out of the glutinous mass and punched it. "*You're* disappointed?"

Molly laughed. "Hey, I'm an old married woman. I have to live vicariously through *somebody.*"

"Well, you won't find much excitement through me, believe me."

Molly walked closer, still clutching her coffee cup and roll. "Nora, what's going on? Is there something you're not telling me?"

Nora stalled. Tipping the huge mound of dough on its side, she twisted and pulled and dug her fingers in, squeezing for all she was worth. She wasn't about to admit, even to Molly, that she was getting hung up on a man she knew darn well was a dead end. Heck, she didn't want to admit that to *herself.*

"There is something."

Before she could surrender to the inquisition and blurt out the truth, a high-pitched wail rose up from the front room. Cocking her head, Nora grinned. "That sounds like Tracy."

"Yep. I'd better go rescue Donna Dixon. Have to take the baby over to Jeff's mom's this morning, anyway." She headed for the swinging door, but before she left, she turned and looked back over her shoulder. "But I still want to know what's going on with you. And I want to hear about tonight's date. So call me, okay?"

As her friend left, Nora nodded. "I'll be sure to tell you everything. As soon as I figure it out myself."

Mike wandered through the darkened house trying not to think about what Nora was doing. Or who she was doing it *with.*

With Emily asleep and the house so quiet it was driving him nuts, he had no distractions to keep his mind from drifting straight to the one woman it shouldn't be drifting to. She would be out on her date with the deputy by now, he thought, stopping in front of the wide front windows.

He looked past his reflection in the glass to the darkness beyond and the images his brain insisted on creating. With no trouble at all, he saw her, in that little black dress she'd worn to the wedding. The one that clung to her every curve and made a man's mouth water at the thought of peeling it off her body. He imagined it clearly, seeing the deputy leaning across a dinner table, smiling into Nora's eyes. He saw him stroke her hand with a lingering touch. He watched as Nora smiled at a man who wasn't *him* and felt his insides tighten into a knot he thought might choke him.

Virgin.

She was a lamb being tossed to the wolves.

What if the deputy got as grabby as Bill Hammond had the night of the wedding? What if Nora said no and the guy didn't listen? What if she needed Mike's help and he was all the way out here, on the ranch?

"That settles it," he muttered, and marched to the telephone on a table beside a sofa. As he hit speed dial and waited for the call to connect, he noticed the

MAUREEN CHILD
93

small vase of flowers and traced the tip of one finger along a fragile petal.

Flowers.

That was Nora's doing.

In the last two weeks, he'd noticed little changes in his house. She brought fresh flowers and dotted the place with them in vases and jars and drinking glasses. She'd bought a few throw pillows to soften the lines of the old leather sofas in the great room. She'd hung curtains and rearranged framed pictures on the wall. She'd brought hair ribbons for Emily and had lately taken to making dinner for the three of them. Her touch was everywhere. She permeated the house. There was no escaping her, even when she wasn't here. Her perfume lingered in the air and taunted his dreams. Her memory danced in his brain and he heard the echoes of her laughter playing over and over again in his mind.

His hand tightened on the receiver when someone picked up the other end and said, ''Hello?''

''Rick, it's me,'' Mike ground out tightly. ''Can you come over here and sit with Emily for a while? I've gotta make a run to town.''

Seth Thomas was a perfectly nice man.

Cute, too.

So why was it, Nora wondered, halfway through

their date, that there were no bells ringing in her mind? No slow sizzle in her blood? No pitch and swirl in the pit of her stomach? She sat across the table from him and listened with half an ear as he told her about the sheriff's academy training program. She nodded in all the right places and gave him an encouraging smile, but the truth of the matter was, she was so not interested. Okay, maybe she wasn't looking to marry Seth. But was a little excitement too much to ask?

What she really wanted to do was go home, put her jammies on and watch an old movie.

Or better yet, go to Mike's house, take her jammies *off* and—she put the mental brakes on that train of thought.

"So," Seth was saying, "when Jeff offered me this job in Tesoro, I grabbed it." He leaned back in his chair and folded his arms across his chest. "Because I think the secret to good law enforcement is…"

She tuned him out again and wondered what Mike was doing right at the moment. Did he miss her? Was he wondering how the date was going?

An hour later, Mike was sitting in his truck outside Nora's house. His gaze locked on the front window, he saw two people through the haze of the curtains. Blurred images, but enough to tell him that Nora had invited her date inside.

Mike's fingers curled around the steering wheel and

squeezed. He should have stayed home. He had no business sitting out here watching her like some damn stalker or something. Nora meant nothing to him. Hell, he'd practically forced her into this date with the new deputy. So he had no one to blame but himself.

But who was talking about blame, here?

Not him.

He was fine.

Just fine.

And firing up the engine, he peeled away from the curb and drove home.

Alone.

Seven

———

"**B**ut he's so cute," Molly said, staring up at Nora as though her best friend was nuts.

"And boring," Nora said with a sigh as she slumped down onto Molly's burgundy-colored sofa. Just thinking about her date last night made her tired. Not that he was a bad guy, but even if it was just about sex then she'd like to go out with a guy who had the ability to heat her blood with a single look. And that wasn't Deputy Thomas. "All night, all he did was tell me about the academy. How he won the fitness medal and that he was top of his sharpshooter class, about how to handcuff a person—"

"Really? Hmm..."

Nora laughed. "Cut it out."

"Just thinking out loud," Molly told her.

"The point is, there was just no..."

"Spark?"

"Exactly," Nora sighed.

"And suddenly you're requiring sparks. I guess I'm not a one night stand kind of woman."

"Well, duh."

Nora shifted uneasily on the couch and let her gaze slide around the room. Cozy, comfortable, Molly's house was cluttered, lived-in. There were fingerprints on the windows, books stacked on tables and a layer of dust on just about everything. Martha Stewart, she wasn't. But as she told anyone who'd listen, she'd have plenty of time to clean house, but her daughter would only be a baby for a little while.

The absolutely perfect Tracy, six months old and growing like...well, okay, a weed, crawled across the toy-strewn floor, gurgling and muttering to herself. Nora's gaze locked on the little sweetheart and her insides ached. The way things were going, she might never have her own children. And the thought of that just made her heartsick.

"Hello?" Molly prompted. "You were saying..."

She glanced at her friend. "I was saying that your daughter gets more gorgeous every day."

Molly practically beamed. "She does, doesn't she?"

But she wasn't distracted for long. Molly had a streak of pit bull in her. "So have you got a spark-worthy someone in mind?"

"Sort of."

"And would this sort of guy be a handsome rancher with a five-year-old daughter?"

Nora's gaze snapped to her friend. "What're you, psychic?"

"Oh, yeah, just call me Molly the Magnificent." Laughing, she propped her feet up on the coffee table. "Honestly, Nora, you've been spending nearly every waking minute with the man for the last two weeks. Who the heck else would it be?"

"For sanity's sake?" Nora countered. "Just about anyone else."

"Mike's a nice guy."

"Oh, he's terrific. He just looks at me and sees Typhoid Mary."

"Okay, this tendency to exaggerate is getting a little out of hand."

"I'm not," Nora said, remembering just how fast Mike had tossed Seth Thomas at her. "He does everything he can to keep me at arm's length."

Molly sat forward and grinned. "If you're at arm's length, honey, he can still reach you."

"Easy for you to say. Jeff melts into a puddle whenever he looks at you."

"Honey, up the temperature and every man will eventually dissolve."

Nora laughed at the thought, though, even as she did, she remembered flashes of heat dazzling Mike's eyes when he looked at her. She recalled standing close beside him and feeling his tension mount until he would stomp off to go somewhere...anywhere, else. Nora smiled to herself and wondered. If she could make him hot enough...maybe even Mike could melt.

The afternoon sun baked the earth and seemed to simmer on Mike's bare back. Heat rippled through him, fueling the fires within that had been raging since the night before. He never should have gone into town. Never should have driven past Nora's place. Never should have tortured himself by imagining her with the deputy.

Because, all night long, his mind had taunted him, drawing up image after image of Nora being kissed and held and touched by someone who wasn't *him*. His grip tightened on the hammer in his right fist. He slammed it against a nail head with enough strength to push it right through the fence plank and out the other side. His right arm sang with the contact, and for one brief second, it took his mind off what he shouldn't be thinking about, anyway.

Small consolation.

When he heard a car pull into the drive, something in the pit of his stomach skittered at the familiar sound of the engine. Mike turned slowly, warily, as if he turned too quickly, that car might disappear. Then he'd be in real trouble. When your imaginings took on solid shape and sound, it was ''rubber room'' time.

The car door opened and Nora climbed out. Sunlight danced on the edges of her hair, making the carelessly tousled mass shine like gold. She looked right at him, as if her gaze had been magnetically drawn to his. Even from across the distance separating them, Mike felt the solid punch of those blue eyes hit him hard and leave him breathless.

She came around the front of the car, all slow moves and a smile, and his gaze swept over her as if he was a blind man who was suddenly given the power to see. He noticed everything about her. A scoop-neck, pale yellow tank top displayed enough creamy, sun-kissed skin on her chest, shoulders and arms to tantalize him. The hem of the darn thing stopped short above the waistband of her grass-green capris, giving him a peek at her belly button and a slash of tanned flesh that made him want to see more. He sucked in a gulp of air, choked it down and kept looking. She wore sandals that displayed that toe ring of hers, and his mouth went dry as he watched her hips sway with each slow, deliberate step toward him.

She didn't stop until she came to the paddock fence. Then she rested her forearms on the top rail, inching the hem of that tank top up a bit more. Mike closed his eyes, hoped for strength, then opened them again to stare directly into hers.

"Who's next?" she asked.

"What?" Blood rushed and pumped through his body, thundering in his ears, and he had to force himself to hear her when she repeated her question.

"I said, who's next on your list?"

He cleared his throat, stuck the claw of the hammer through one of his belt loops and walked toward her. Damned if he'd let her know what just looking at her was doing to him. "What list?"

"You know, prospective deflowerers," Nora said. She tipped her head to one side and asked, "Is that even a word?"

Who cared? "What are you talking about?" He deliberately kept his gaze locked with hers. Way less dangerous than allowing himself another glimpse of tanned, creamy skin.

She smiled and it sucker punched him.

"C'mon, Mike. Seth Thomas couldn't have been your best shot."

The knot that had been lodged in the center of his chest since the night before slowly dissolved. "Didn't like him?"

"Oh, he's nice," she said, "but when push came to shove—or rather when touch came to pawing..."

"He *pawed* you?"

"That was the idea, wasn't it?" She shifted and ran her fingertips along the edge of the fence rail. "I mean, I can't really lose the whole virginity banner unless some touching is involved."

"Right." His gaze slipped and followed the languorous movement of her fingers until he clenched his jaw and had to look away again.

"But it just didn't feel..." She shrugged, and the clingy material of her blouse tightened across her breasts.

"You know?"

All he knew for sure was, if he didn't get the hell away from her, damn fast, she wouldn't have to worry about finding somebody to "deflower" her. She'd be flat on her back in the paddock, with him right on top of her.

That image flashed into his mind and held there, freeze-framed.

"Mike?" Nora said, waving one hand in front of his face.

"Yeah!" He snapped out of it instantly, shook his head and blew out a rush of air.

"You okay?"

"Fine," he muttered, and snatched his hat off to stab his fingers through his hair. At least, he would be fine as soon as he could find enough cold water to soak his body in. The Arctic Ocean ought to be big enough.

"Well, you don't look okay," Nora said, inwardly smiling. Ah, it was good to know that even if she wasn't much of a flirt, she was girl enough to bring a man to his knees. Figuratively, if not literally. Feigning concern, she suggested, "Maybe you've had too much sun today."

"I'm fine," he insisted.

"It's really hot, though," she said on a soft moan, tilting her head back and stroking her neck with the tips of her fingers. "Feels like my skin's on fire."

He inhaled slowly, deeply. She heard the deliberate intake of air, and it did her a world of good to know that he was totally affected by her.

"I gotta get back to work," he said tightly, and turned away, headed back for the far side of the paddock.

"Oh, okay then," Nora said, shifting her gaze to meet his. "I'll just go on inside and say hi to Emily."

He stopped dead and half turned to look at her over his shoulder. "You're staying?"

"Sure," she said, smiling at him. "We've still got to find me a man, don't we?" Then she spun around and walked toward the house, intentionally swaying her hips in what she hoped was a provocative move. She felt his gaze on her as she walked, and if she'd been made of straw, she'd have burst into flame from the heat of his stare. As it was, her skin hummed, her insides churned, her knees wobbled and places in her body that had yet to be introduced to passion sat up and begged.

So just *who* was torturing *whom* here?

Mike stayed outside working as long as he could, but, eventually, he had to give it up and go inside. Rick was spending more and more time with Donna, as he should be, Mike thought. But that meant more work for him and less time with Emily.

So, he should be grateful that Nora had come back, right? At least his daughter was happy and well-looked-after. What did it really matter, in the grand scheme of things, that he was going slowly insane?

He stepped into the kitchen, hung his hat on the wall peg and looked around the empty room. A casserole dish, covered with foil, sat on the stove top. Dishes had been washed and put away, but there was a single place setting, for him, waiting on the table. Apparently Emily and Nora had already eaten.

And despite the fact that he'd stayed out late on purpose, he was disappointed to realize he'd missed dinner with them. The clock over the sink read seven-fifteen and Mike felt a stab of guilt. Nearly Emily's bedtime and he'd hardly seen her all day. He could

take care of that, though. Just grab a quick shower
and—

"Mike?"

Nora's voice, coming from the great room.

He got a grip on his hormones and walked through
the doorway and down the hall. "Yeah, I just came in
and—" He stopped as he entered the room. Emily lay
on one of the sofas, cuddled up beneath a blanket.
Nora was sitting right beside her.

Worry and fear roared to life inside him as he
crossed the room in a few long strides. Dropping to
one knee beside his daughter, he looked up into Nora's
worried gaze and asked, "What's wrong?"

She shook her head and shrugged. "I don't know.
She was fine a few minutes ago and now—"

"Daddy—" Emily's voice came soft and tired "—I
don't feel good."

"What hurts, baby?" he asked, his tone gentle,
crooning as he stroked her bangs back from her forehead. "Your tummy?"

"No," she whined, and cupped one small hand
around her neck. "My froat's sore."

"Mike, I swear," Nora was saying, and he heard
the tension in her voice, "up until a few minutes ago,
she was fine. We were coloring." She waved one hand
at the abandoned coloring books and crayons lying
scattered across the coffee table.

"Kids get sick fast," he muttered, and spared a

quick look at the beautiful blonde beside him. "Don't worry about it."

"Daddy, it hu-u-urts...."

Despite the concern washing through him, Mike could still appreciate how a kid was able to shove three syllables into a one-syllable word. "It's okay, baby. Daddy'll fix it."

Emily closed her eyes and turned onto her side, curling up into a tiny cocoon. Mike bent down, planted a kiss on the top of her head and stood up, motioning Nora to follow him as he moved across the room. She did, reluctantly, continually glancing back at the child lying so uncharacteristically still.

"Nora," he said, and she focused on him. "Look, I don't want to ask, but I'm filthy. Will you stay with Emily while I take a quick shower? Then I'll take over caring for Emily and you can go home."

She looked at him as if he had two heads. "I'm not going anywhere," she said after a long minute of stunned silence.

"You don't have to stay," he said tightly. "Emily's had these before. It's just a sore throat. I just have to keep her fever down. She'll be fine."

"I'm sure she will," Nora agreed, folding her arms beneath her breasts and shooting him a look that told him she was going to be stubborn about this. "And I'll be right here with her to see it for myself."

"No-o-ora" came a soft wail from the couch, "read to me...."

Nora winced slightly and sympathy shone in her eyes as she called back, "I'll be right there, sweetie." Then, turning back to Mike, she lowered her voice and added, "Go ahead. Get cleaned up. Have dinner. And get used to me. Because I'm not leaving her."

Then before he could argue, or tell her that he could take care of his own child, Nora was gone, hurrying back to the sofa. Picking up Emily's favorite book, she began to read, and the sound of her voice—calm, loving, gentle—filled the room. Mike simply stood in the shadows, watching the two of them. He was still standing there when Emily reached out and Nora folded that tiny hand in hers.

A pang of something sweet and just a little terrifying ricocheted around the inside of his heart. It had been just he and Emily for so long, he wasn't used to sharing the care of her. But clearly, his little girl had found something in Nora that she needed. Responded to.

And that worried him. Because eventually, Nora would leave and what would that do to Emily?

Two hours later, Nora was a wreck. All thoughts of hot seduction were long since banished from her mind and every ounce of her concentration was focused on Emily. She looked so small, so helpless, lying in her bed surrounded by her stuffed animals. The little girl's cheeks were flushed and her eyes held the glassy sheen of a fever.

"Read it again," she whispered, and the scratchy sound of her voice brought a sympathetic ache to Nora's throat.

"Okay, sweetie," she said, and drew the child in close, wrapping her arm around her. Emily nestled her head on Nora's chest, and even through the fabric of her shirt, Nora felt the heat radiating from the small body pressed close to her.

Worry tugged at her heart and tore at the edges of her mind. But she read the storybook one more time, trying to keep Emily's mind off her own misery. And while she read the story about a sick little bunny and his friends, Nora concentrated on the feel of Emily's slight body curled into hers. Though she hated that the child was sick, Nora loved feeling needed, loved that Emily felt comforted by her presence.

"Will I still be sick on Friday?"

Nora stopped reading and shifted her gaze to the wide blue eyes looking up at her. "I don't know, honey, why?"

"'Cuz Mandy in my class is having her birthday and we get to sleep over at her house and everything." Emily's bottom lip curled and one fat tear slipped from her left eye and rolled along her cheek.

"Aw, sweetie, don't cry...."

"Who's crying?" Mike asked.

Nora turned to look at the doorway, where Mike stood, leaning against the jamb, hands in his jeans pockets, bare feet crossed at the ankle.

How long had he been standing there?

"Me, Daddy," Emily said as more tears joined the first one.

He smiled softly and pushed away from the door, walking into the room to take a seat across from Nora, next to Emily. "Don't worry about the party, baby," he said softly, and ran his fingertips along her cheek. "You'll be okay by then."

"Really?" A half smile curved her mouth.

"Really. Now, why don't you try to sleep, okay?"

"'Kay," she said, and cuddled in closer to Nora.

Mike watched her and shook his head. "Maybe you should lie down?"

"Nora's readin' to me."

"Yeah," Nora said, smiling. "I'm readin' to her."

One corner of Mike's mouth tilted into a smile that set off firecrackers deep inside Nora. She felt the pop and sizzle of them as they scattered, throughout her bloodstream. Pulling in a long, slow breath, she forced her gaze from his and looked instead at the pages of the book she could barely see through the haze of desire clouding her vision.

How did he do that? How did he look at her and

make her want to rip her clothes off and throw herself at him?

"Mind if I listen, too?" he asked, his voice a low rumble of sound that rippled along her spine and settled into an ache deep inside her.

"You can cuddle with Nora, too, Daddy," Emily offered.

Nora sucked in a gulp of air.

Mike heard her.

And gave her a look that made her head spin.

In a good way.

Eight

Emily was sound asleep and her fever was down. But Nora still refused to leave. Mike watched her from the hall doorway, and in the soft glow of the princess night-light gleaming in the corner of the room, she looked...too damn good.

He leaned forward, bracing his hands on either side of the doorway and squeezed until he wouldn't have been surprised to hear the old wood snap in his grip. To indulge himself, he let his gaze slide over her. That fresh-as-a-daisy outfit she'd been wearing when she arrived was now wrinkled and stained with a few drops of liquid ibuprofen. She'd raked her hands

through her hair so often it was a tangled mess, and
her eyes looked tired and worried.

Still, desire flashed inside him, even brighter and
stronger than it had that afternoon. This was more than
a reaction to her good looks, though God knew that
was there, too. He was responding to who she *was*.
How she'd cared for Emily. How she'd worried and
fretted and read one story time after time until he was
pretty sure she knew it by heart.

This desire raging and pulsing inside him was fu-
eled by what he'd seen of her in the last few weeks.
It was the flowers in his house. The laughter that had
brightened every corner of a home that had grown too
dark. The warmth that had invaded his soul no matter
how much he tried to fight it.

And he knew there would be no relief from the
wanting because he couldn't give her what she was
looking for. Couldn't take that kind of risk. If he only
had to consider his own happiness, then he might surrender to these feelings. But he had Emily to think
about, too. And to protect her from another possible
rejection, he would do anything. Even if it meant de-
nying himself the one woman he wanted more than
his next breath.

As if she sensed him watching her, she shifted her
gaze to him. When their gazes locked, Mike knew he
was in deep trouble. She stood up, bent down and

stroked Emily's forehead, then straightened again and moved across the room.

Mike stepped aside as she got closer. When she passed him, she brushed against his body and his skin caught fire. That was the only explanation for the sudden explosion of heat that damn near swamped him. Shaking his head, he gave his sleeping daughter one last look, then turned and followed Nora out into the great room.

She kept walking until she stood in front of the now-cold hearth. On the mantel above the stone fireplace was a line of framed photos. Most were of Emily, but there were a few others, too.

"Are these your parents?" she asked without turning around.

"Yeah," he said, and stopped a good five feet from her. Couldn't hurt to keep a little distance between them. "They live up north. Near Reno."

"Pretty up there," she said, and let her fingers trail along the oak mantel, sliding up to the next picture. "And this?"

"My sister," he said, shoving his hands into his jeans pockets. "She and her family live in Montana."

"You're spread out far and wide, aren't you?"

"Just worked out that way." But his family had never really been close, anyway. Oh, they visited, called and e-mailed. But tight, they weren't.

"That's a shame," she mused, her voice quiet,

thoughtful. "My family drives me nuts occasionally, but I can't imagine not having them close by."

"I have Emily."

"And she's enough?"

"She's everything."

Finally, Nora turned to look at him. There were tears in her eyes, and since he hadn't been expecting it, those tears hit him hard. He took a step toward her, then stopped again, unsure just what to do. Damn it, tears always threw him for a loop.

She used both hands to swipe her cheeks dry, then sniffed and gulped in air like a drowning woman. Shaking her head, she gave him a watery smile and said, "She is everything to you. I can see that when you're together."

She took another deep, shuddering breath and continued. "I envy you that, you know?"

What was he supposed to say to that? he wondered. *Thank you?*

But she didn't give him a chance to think of something to say. Instead, she kept talking, her words rushing from her, tumbling over one another into a long, blurred stream of sound. He listened hard, straining to keep up, to hear everything.

"I watched you with her and you were so good, so gentle, and you knew exactly what to do and you weren't scared. You weren't worried. I saw your eyes," she said, wagging a finger at him as if accusing him of something dire. "You weren't worried. Concerned, maybe, but not scared. I was so scared, I didn't know what to do. She got that fever in just a few minutes. It came up out of nowhere and…" She shrugged, threw her hands high and then let them slap down to her sides again. "If you hadn't walked in the door when you did, I would have been running out into the dark to find you. I was terrified. I mean, I've been sick and that's no biggie. I can take aspirin and tuck myself into bed. But watching Emily cry and seeing her face flushed and her eyes go all glassy…" She cringed even at the memory. "It was terrible. I felt so helpless. So stupid. How can you deal with that so easily? How do you watch a kid be perfectly healthy one minute and then sick in the next?"

"Nora…" Eventually, he had to try to stop the flow of words. Her tears were running again, coursing down her cheeks in a flood of misplaced guilt.

"My God," she whispered as her voice wound down into a hoarse echo of what it had been, "I have no business wanting a family. Kids of my own? If I react like this, what good would I be to them? I mean, what if they fell and cut themselves? Would I faint at the sight of blood? Would I just sit on the floor and cry with them?" She pushed her hands through her hair. "Yeah, I'm the one you want around in a crisis."

"That's bull."

"What?" Her head snapped up and her gaze shot to his.

Mike looked at her and felt his heart squeeze at the sight of her tear-streaked face and misery-filled eyes. He just couldn't stand it another minute. In three long strides, he was beside her. Grabbing her upper arms in a firm yet gentle grip, he drew her up onto her toes and stared deeply into her eyes.

He felt a tremor race through her body and skip into his. This close, her eyes looked as blue as a lake— and just as fathomless. She chewed at her bottom lip in a ridiculous attempt to stem the tears that were still raining down her face. Her breath came in short, hard gulps.

He squeezed her arms a bit tighter and said again, "It's bull, Nora. All of it. At least," he said with a shake of his head, "what I caught of that monologue. You talk so damn fast, it's hard to be sure."

A tremulous smile flitted across her face and was gone again in an instant. "My mom always said that when I was nervous she couldn't hear a word I was saying."

"I know what she meant," he grumbled. "But the upshot of this is, you're blaming yourself because you panicked."

"Exactly," she said, and tried to worm out of his grasp. But there was no way someone as small as Nora was going to get away from Mike if he didn't want her to. And damn it, he didn't.

"You didn't panic, Nora. You took care of her. You read to her. The same damn story over and over until I would have pulled my hair out in frustration." He gave her a small smile and was rewarded with one just like it.

"That's not true," she said, leaning into him. "Emily already told me you read her that story every night."

"Wrong," he said on a sigh, enjoying too much the feel of her body pressed along his. "I *recite* it. I learned it by heart months ago."

She laughed. The sound was hesitant, unsure, but it was there, however briefly.

Mike's gaze swept over her face, her hair, and came back to her eyes. So deep. So blue. So…innocent. Hell, he never would have believed that in the twenty-first century, you could find an *innocent* over the age of fifteen. Yet here she stood.

In his arms.

His thumbs moved back and forth over her bare arms, and the feel of her skin beneath his sent a rush of fire pouring through him. His body tightened and breathing became a real issue.

But he wasn't holding her for his own satisfaction, right? He was supposed to be consoling her. He got back to the subject at hand and tried to tell his body to chill out.

"Kids get sick fast, Nora. But they heal just as quick, most of the time." He shrugged helplessly. "And, nine times out of ten, all you can do is stand there and watch over them. Try to make them more comfortable."

Her gaze dropped.

He dipped his head to reestablish the connection. "*Read* to them."

She smiled again.

"You did good."

Nora sucked in a long deep gulp of air and blew it out again, ruffling the stray curl draped over her forehead. "If you're lying to make me feel better," she said, "I want you to know you're doing a great job."

His mouth quirked. "I'm not lying."

She studied his features for a long minute, as if trying to read the truth in his expression. What she saw must have convinced her finally because she nodded and whispered, "Thanks."

"No problem." His thumbs moved over her skin again, and this time she shivered and he felt her reaction kick around inside him. Deliberately, his grip loosened as he told himself to take a step back. That they were too close, standing here in the dimly lit room. Moonlight streamed through the uncurtained front windows and lay in a silvery pattern on the worn rugs and hardwood floors.

The one lamp burning in the room cast a small circle of golden light that came nowhere near them as they stood locked together near the hearth.

"Mike…" she whispered, and her voice seemed to dance at the back of his neck, sending every damn one of his nerve endings onto red alert.

While he still could, Mike let her go and took a half step backward. Scrubbing one hand across his face, he told himself to ignore her perfume—some delicate flowery scent—as it surrounded him, filling the air with a power that threatened to rock him to his knees. "Look," he said tightly, remembering that there was no future in this, "Emily's asleep. She's going to be fine by morning. Maybe you should be headed home."

"I don't want to leave just yet," she said, and took a step closer.

Now, she might be a virgin, but Mike certainly wasn't, and he'd seen that determined look on a woman's face before. She'd made up her mind about something, and he had a feeling that once Nora had set her course it would take more than logic to change it.

"Nora, this isn't a good idea," he said, feeling it only fair that he try, anyway, despite the low chance of success.

"See," she said, coming even closer, "that's where you're wrong, cowboy. I think it's a great idea."

And then she was in his arms, pressing her body into his, wrapping her arms around his neck and going up on her toes until their mouths were just a kiss apart.

Mike's body went hard and tight. Every muscle, every cell, sizzled and burned. He clenched his jaw and fought against grabbing her. His hands fisted at his sides even as he felt his blood boil.

Her breath dusted his face. Her fingers stroked through his hair and he felt her touch right down to his bones. She shifted a little, rubbing her abdomen against him. She smiled knowingly.

"You know, Mike, I think you think it's a better idea than you think you do."

He blinked, shook his head and ground out, *"What?"*

"Oh," she said, running the tip of one finger around the inside collar of his dark red T-shirt. "I think you understand me."

He shuddered and, in self defense, grabbed her tight, holding her still, with his arms locked around her waist and tightening like a vise.

"Oomph." Her breath was squeezed from her lungs, but it didn't seem to be bothering her any.

"Nora," Mike said, forcing his voice to work around the huge knot of need lodged in his throat, "I'm not the one you want."

She tipped her head to one side and gave him a crooked smile that stabbed right to the heart of him. "How do you know what I want, cowboy?"

"Quit calling me that," he grumbled. "I'm a rancher."

"You're a cowboy," she murmured, and let her fingers trail through his hair again, sending tiny lightning bolts blasting throughout his body.

"I'm not gonna do this."

"Oh, I think you will."

Damn it, he thought. She was way more right than he was.

"C'mon cowboy," she murmured, moving her mouth even closer to his. "Be a hero, kiss the girl."

His right hand swept up her spine. Threading his fingers through her fine, silky blond hair, he cupped the back of her head and held her still for one long, heart-stopping second. Staring down into her blue eyes, he felt himself fall, and the last rational thought that darted through his brain was *What the hell. What harm can one kiss do?*

"Yes ma'am," he muttered, and took her mouth in a fiery kiss that slammed into both of them with the strength and raw fury of a runaway train.

Nora held on tight and enjoyed this new experience. She'd been on a roller-coaster ride of emotions all night. First teasing Mike, then sitting beside Emily's sickbed, then here again, in the dark, with Mike. Talking to him, watching him, feeling the power of his forest-green eyes were all enough to send any healthy woman over the edge.

But seeing him in action as a tender, loving father had just topped off what she'd felt building inside her for weeks now. Mike Fallon was more man than she'd ever hoped to find. Her body hummed when he was around. She hated leaving him at night and couldn't wait to see him again. Was that love? She didn't know. Didn't want to think about it. At least not now. For now, all she wanted to do was *feel*.

She'd saved herself for years, hoping, praying the one special man might come along. Then, she'd given up hope. Now, here, tonight, she'd found him.

The fact that he wasn't interested in love or forever was something she'd worry about tomorrow. Tonight, she wanted his arms around her. She wanted to taste and feel and experience everything she'd been missing all these years.

His mouth opened over hers, his tongue parting her lips, sweeping into her mouth to dazzle her even further. She'd been kissed before, her brain screamed out, but her body knew better. She might have been kissed, but she'd never been *kissed*.

And Mike was a man with a real gift for kissing.

She groaned softly as he took more of her, tasting, exploring, delving deep into the heart of her. His breath brushed her cheek, his tongue entwined with hers, dazzling her, stealing her breath and sending her pulse beat into a rapid dance that pounded in her ears and left her shivering.

Again and again, he explored her, while his hands moved up and down her back, along her curves, finding their way along her body, driving the heat swamping her into an inferno. Nora held on to him, clinging to his broad shoulders as if her life depended on him.

Dazzling fireworks exploded behind her closed eyes, and the falling sparks seemed to shatter and spill throughout her body. Her brain shut down, but that didn't matter. No thought was necessary. She forgot to breathe and didn't care. Everything else in the world fell away as she stood wrapped in the center of his warm, solid strength. She wanted that kiss to go on and on. She wanted his hands on her body, and the fire inside quickened until she felt flushed from head to toe. Still, she wanted more.

A moment later, he broke the kiss, dragging his mouth from hers. She struggled for air and rested her head on his chest, trying to get her balance back, comforting herself with the ragged beat of his heart. Standing on her own two feet again, she swayed into him, afraid that if he moved away too quickly, she'd fall flat on her face.

Noodly knees would do that to a person.

He drew in a long, deep breath and let it shudder

through him as he rested his chin on top of her head. "Nora, do us both a favor and go home. Now."

"I don't think I can walk," she confessed.

"I'll carry you to your car."

She leaned her head back to stare up at him. When she saw the dark swirl of desire gleaming in his eyes, her knees went weak again. "Mike, you don't want me to leave. I can see it in your eyes."

"What I want and what I'm going to do are two different things."

Disappointment welled inside her. "They don't have to be."

"Yeah," he said, "they do." And he let her go, taking a step back that was as much mental as it was physical. She felt him withdraw, pull away from the closeness they'd just shared. Nora wanted to kick him.

"You can just shut it off. Just like that." Shaking her head, she glared at him and tried not to think about the fact that her mouth was still humming, her blood still racing.

"If you think this is easy, you're nuts."

"Then why do it?" she demanded, anger and frustration coloring her voice.

"Because one of us has to think clearly."

"Ahhh…" she said on a long, slow inhalation. She dropped both hands to her hips, tapped her left foot against the rug beneath her and snapped, "So what you're saying is, you'll do the thinking for the poor, weak little female who doesn't know her own mind?''

His jaw tightened, the muscle twitching spasmodically. ''I didn't say that.''

''Sure you did, Mike.'' In a slow, measured walk, she moved in a circle around him, forcing him to turn his head just to keep his eye on her. ''You're so tall and strong and smart and everything. And you've had sex…at least *once,* for sure.''

''Hey…''

''So of course you should take charge here, right?''

''I didn't say I was—''

''So, yeah, Mike. Fine. I'll leave, because I'm not really feeling romantic anymore, anyway, in case you didn't guess that by the way I'm talking and how fast the words are coming out—''

His features tight, he muttered, ''I got it, but—''

''But you know something?'' Nora said, moving close enough to poke her index finger into his chest with the force of a nail being pounded into a piece of oak. ''You're going to regret this, Mike.'' She moved in closer still, keeping her gaze locked with his, then, her voice low and husky with choked-off need, she whispered, ''When you're lying there alone in your bed tonight, Mike, I want you to remember that you sent me home.'' She ran her fingers down the front of his shirt, then fisted her hands in the material, pulling his head down to hers. "You'll miss me, cowboy. You know you will."

Then she kissed him, hard, slanting her mouth over his and pouring everything she was feeling into that one, last kiss. She felt him give, surrender to the moment, and when his hands came up to her back, she let him go and moved out of his reach. It was small consolation that he looked like he'd been hit on the head.

"This is over for tonight, cowboy," she said, mustering what little dignity she could. Lifting her chin, she met his gaze coolly. "But *just* for tonight."

Then, with her insides churning and her brain spinning, she left him standing there in the dim light and didn't look back.

Nine

"You've got to set the hook and reel him in." Nora's mother glanced at her briefly, then turned her gaze back to the crochet project on her lap.

"Exactly," Frannie piped up, and wiped her baby's drooly chin.

"Honestly, Nora," Jenny complained, hefting her daughter up to her shoulder to be burped. "How have you managed to live this long without knowing the game?"

Nora's gaze drifted from one member of her family to the next. Her mom, Rose, sat in a wing chair with sunlight pouring over her shoulder and onto the spill of garnet yarn cascading off her lap to pool at her feet. Frannie and Jenny were each busy with their kids, but apparently still had plenty of time to give Nora the advice they were so sure she desperately needed.

The house where she grew up hadn't changed much over the years. Oh, it had newer furniture and the carpet had been replaced once or twice. The absence of her father was still felt five years after his passing. But, basically, it was the same old comfortable Victorian. Where she came every two weeks to be harassed over lunch whether she needed it or not.

For the last half hour, the hot topic of discussion was her relationship—or lack thereof—with Mike Fallon. Apparently, the whole darn town was talking about her and Mike. Not so surprising, really. There wasn't a lot going on in Tesoro, so having a new piece of gossip was almost enough reason to throw a carnival. With Nora spending as much time with Mike as she had in the last few weeks, it was no wonder people were speculating.

"Who says you have to play games?" she suddenly asked of no one in particular.

All three of them snorted muffled laughs.

Gritting her teeth, Nora defended her position. "Game playing is for kids. Men and women should be honest with each other."

"Ah, so speaks the still unattached sister," Frannie muttered.

"Wisdom from the virgin goddess." Jenny rolled her eyes and congratulated her little daughter on a burp well done.

Nora gritted her teeth, but before she could shoot back some pithy retort, another voice interrupted.

"You girls stop it," their mother said, and Nora shifted her gaze to the woman with softly graying blond hair. "Nora, honey, what works for some doesn't necessarily work for others." Pulling a stitch tight, she laid her silver hook down and rested her hands in her lap. Smiling, she continued. "You've always been as honest as the day is long, Nora. No sense in trying to change now."

"Thank you, Mom," she said, giving her sisters a meaningful look.

"But," Rose said quickly, drawing her daughter's gaze back to hers. "Honesty surely isn't always the easiest policy when dealing with a man."

"Amen," Frannie muttered.

Their mother ignored her and focused on Nora. "Pay no attention, honey. What I'm trying to say is, it won't be easy, but if you want Mike, then you have to figure out how to convince him of that in your own way." She leaned forward, bracing her elbows on her knees, and smiled at her eldest daughter. "I know you, Nora. Where you love, you love strong and deep. If this is really love, then go for it, honey. Find your own way and do what you think best."

Tears stung the backs of Nora's eyes as she looked into her mother's warm, soft blue gaze. It was good, she thought, to have a place where you were known so well. Where, no matter what, you belonged and people understood.

"Really, Nora, all you have to do is make up your mind and then convince him that his mind is made up, too." Jenny grinned at her from across the room.

Now, that sounded so much easier than it was probably going to be, Nora thought.

"Oh!" Frannie squealed. "Look. Look." She pointed at her little son. The eleven-month-old had pulled himself to his feet. While the women in the room held their collected breaths, tiny hands fisted in the fabric of the sofa cushion. And with his proud family looking on, little Jake took his first toddling steps.

When he dropped onto his well-padded bottom, his delighted mother scooped him up, cheering for his victory. Nora sat on the floor, watching her sisters and her mother congratulating the little boy. Tears filled her eyes, and she felt a raw, open tide of love rush through her, so thick, so powerful, it nearly choked her.

Family.

That's what mattered.

That's what she wanted most.

And she knew just what she had to do to get it.

* * *

Things were getting back to normal.

At least, that's what Mike kept telling himself. He hadn't seen Nora in nearly two days. Not since she'd set his body on fire and then walked out of his house to let him burn to a crisp alone.

"Just as well," he said, throwing Emily's sleeping bag and balloon-decorated overnight case into the back of the truck. Nora had obviously finally accepted that whatever there was between them just wasn't going to go any further.

"Hey, boss!"

Mike's head jerked up and he squinted into the afternoon sunlight to watch Rick approach. "What's up?"

Rick shook his head and snapped his thumb toward his own house at the other end of the ranch yard. "You coming right back from town?"

"Yeah. Be gone about a half hour."

"Excellent. On your way back, will you stop and pick up some tacos for Donna?"

Mike smiled to himself. "Thought she was craving ice cream?"

"Last week," Rick said on a sigh. "This week, it's tacos."

"Sure, I'll get 'em."

"Thanks," Rick said, already heading for the barn. "I owe you."

''No problem,'' Mike said, remembering all too well what it was like to deal with a pregnant wife. Of course, Vicky had pretty much resented the whole situation. She'd complained for nine long months. She'd hated the changes in her body. Hated the baby. Most especially, though, she'd hated *Mike* for creating the child in the first place.

And as long and miserable as that pregnancy had been, none of it had mattered the minute the nurse handed his new daughter to him. Mike could still see Emily—tiny, red, screaming her head off. It was still a moment he thought of as miraculous. Hell, he'd had just about had *sucker* stamped on his forehead from the moment he took his first look at his little girl.

He'd always wanted three or four kids. He smiled at the thought of the ranch ringing with the sound of squeals and laughter. But, an instant later, that smile disappeared as he reminded himself that Emily would be his one and only child. And that was a shame, he admitted, if only to himself. Mike hadn't counted on living the rest of his life alone. He'd wanted a wife. A big family.

But he'd messed it all up so badly, so completely, that he figured he'd had his shot and blown it. Now it wasn't his turn to go out and try to find happiness. He wouldn't let Emily care about someone else, only to be abandoned again. His daughter had to be his pri-

ority. Now it was Emily's turn. And he'd do everything he could to make sure his little girl was happy.

Nora had a plan.

She'd even called in the big guns. Making Jenny
and Frannie go shopping with her, she'd picked out
lingerie that was so sexy she was half surprised it
hadn't burned a hole right through the bag she'd carried it home in. With her hair and nails done, she felt
pampered and pretty and, let's face it…ready to do
battle.

She only wished her nerves were as rock steady as
her eyeliner. Her stomach swirled with what felt like
hundreds of butterflies, and her mouth was so dry it
hurt to swallow.

Inhaling sharply, deeply, she muttered encourage-
ment to herself. "Come on, Nora. You can do this."
She laid the flat of her hand at the base of her throat
and picked up the staccato beat of her own pulse.
Okay, the plan wouldn't get a chance to work if she
passed out before she even got started.

She stared through her windshield at the ranch
house sitting dark and silent at the end of the drive.
A single light in the kitchen told her exactly where
Mike was in the big old house—and her heartbeat
quickened even further. He was alone. Tonight was
Emily's big sleepover party.

Nora swallowed again and tried to steady her

breathing. She steered the car down the drive, following the twin slashes from her headlights. The now familiar sound of gravel crunching beneath her tires seemed...welcoming, somehow. Parking the car, she grabbed her purse and climbed out, closing the door behind her.

She shot a quick look at Rick and Donna's little house and was reassured to see several lights on, plus the flickering of a TV set. There would be no interruptions from that quarter. Now all she needed was to find the nerve to carry out the plan.

The kitchen door opened and a slice of yellow light stabbed through the darkness, silhouetting Mike standing in the doorway. He looked huge. Tall, broad shouldered and exactly what she wanted.

"Nora?" he said, and his voice, though low pitched, carried easily in the quiet she'd learned to appreciate out here, so far from Tesoro.

"Surprise."

He stepped out onto the porch and the light fell on him. With his features half in shadow, he looked mysterious, untouchable. A part of Nora wanted to just say "forget the whole thing" and go home, but she'd come too far to back out now. Besides, that tiny, cowardly voice in the back of her mind was easy to ignore, buried as it was beneath the roaring of her own blood.

"I didn't expect to see you out here again," he said, and folded both arms across his chest.

She came around the front of the car and stepped carefully on the gravel as she felt her high heels wobble unsteadily. The cool night air slipped up beneath the hem of the knee-length linen coat she wore belted around her waist and sent a shiver up the length of her spine. But she was pretty sure it wasn't only the air making her feel the tingle of goose bumps on her skin.

"We should talk," she said softly, stepping up onto the porch to stand alongside him. The three-inch heels made her nearly tall enough to look him square in the eye. Nora noticed that despite his lack of welcome, there was a flash of…something in his eyes that gave her the courage to take the next step.

Pulling in a deep breath, she moved past him into the well-worn kitchen. A white take-out bag sat in the middle of the table. The scent of Mexican spices filled the air, and Nora smiled to herself as she looked around the big room. It was homey and familiar and about to become the site of Nora's first attempt at seduction.

"If you're here to talk about the other night…" he started.

"No," she said, cutting him off as she dropped her purse onto the table and turned to face him. "I'm here to talk about tonight."

Mike kept his distance. For all the good it did him. Just seeing her here again was enough to stir up every ounce of the desire he'd spent the last two days trying to ignore. Her short blond hair was softly curled and fell around her face in a wild, tangled halo. Her blue eyes looked dark, smoky and dangerous as hell. She was wearing those strappy high heels that had looked so good on her the night of the wedding. And even her pale blue linen coat looked sexy belted tight around her narrow waist.

A coat, though? Spring evenings were cool, but not cold enough to warrant bundling up.

Not the point, he told himself. The main thing here was to get Nora out of the house before—

Her hands dropped to the knotted belt at her waist and he watched as she tugged at it. Apparently she planned on staying awhile.

"What are you doing?"

"Setting the stage for our little talk."

"The stage?" he asked, and before he could figure out what she meant exactly, Nora shrugged out of the coat to let it fall to the floor.

Mike's heart stopped.

Under that simple linen coat she was wearing the most amazing combination of silk and lace he'd ever seen. Red-wine-colored silk caressed her body, skimming along her skin, hugging her curves before ending in a short skirt that just covered the tops of her thighs. Slender straps smoothed across her shoulders and across her breasts; the silk gave way to a fragile lace that managed to both hide and display her breasts. Her legs looked long and lean and tanned and his hands itched to touch her, to explore every inch of her.

Reaching out blindly, he slammed the back door closed and wished he had curtains to close, too. "Oh, man."

"You like it?" she asked, and Mike thought that had to be the dumbest question he'd ever heard.

He sucked in air through gritted teeth and finally lifted his gaze to hers. "Like it? Yeah, I guess you could say that."

"Good." Her mouth, that fabulous mouth, curved in a soft smile that let Mike know she was completely aware of the effect she was having on him.

She did a slow, lazy turn in a tight circle, giving him enough time to appreciate her from every angle. And damned if she didn't look fantastic from every angle. His body went tight and hard. His blood pumped viciously and his heartbeat raced until he was sure it would jump right out of his chest.

"I was hoping you'd like it. Sort of makes up for standing here freezing."

"Nora—"

She met his gaze and tilted her head to one side to look at him. "You're not going to try to tell me to leave, are you, Mike?"

"Would it work?" he ground out tightly.

"Not a chance." She moved a little closer to him, and damned if he could convince himself to back up.

Her scent reached him first. That delicate blend of flowers that he would know in the dark and be able to find her by following it.

Oh, man.

"But you could warm me up a little."

"Warm?" A strained, harsh laugh shot from his throat. "Honey, if you're not careful, you're gonna end up in the middle of a forest fire."

Her eyes flashed and her lips parted in a half smile that fed the flames licking at his insides. Mike knew he was a dead man. There was just no way he could let her go. No way he could face the rest of this night without touching her. No way he could last another ten seconds without having her.

"That's why I'm here, Mike," she said, and came close enough to skim her hands up his chest.

His body flashed with an inner heat. Her hands went up, wrapped around his neck and her fingers threaded through his hair. A low grumble of need and want erupted inside him and Mike fought to keep it under control. To keep from losing himself.

"I want you," she said. "I want you to make love to me, Mike."

"Nora, this is crazy."

She nodded, never taking her gaze off his. "I know. It has been right from the start."

"I'm not the man you need."

"You're exactly the man I want, though."

He sucked in another gulp of air and released it in a rush of frustration. Grabbing her around the waist, he slid his fingers along her silk-clad body and felt her tremble at his touch.

She went up on her toes and planted a quick kiss at the corner of his mouth, and he felt himself weaken even further. He'd been fighting this for weeks. Desire had become a constant companion, and frustration a way of life. Well, damn it, a man could take just so much.

"Nora, are you sure?"

She actually laughed, and he watched her eyes dazzle with pleasure. "Are you kidding? I dressed up like this, drove out to your house, stripped in your kitchen and you're asking if I'm *sure?* Jeez, Mike, I'm practically attacking you."

His mouth quirked into a half smile. She had a point.

Nora kissed him then, long and hard and deep, and when it was finally over, she pulled her head back to look at him. "Well, cowboy?"

Shaking his head, Mike told himself that by tomorrow, he'd probably be able to think of hundreds of reasons why he shouldn't be doing this. But tonight he couldn't even think of one.

Still holding her at the waist, he shifted his grip, scooped her up into his arms, and when she laughed in delight, he told himself not to think beyond tonight.

To take this time with Nora as a gift and not question it.

"Hang on, little lady," he said in his best cowboy drawl, "it's gonna be a long night."

"Promises, promises." Nora laughed and wrapped her arms around his neck as he stalked across the kitchen and through the house to his bedroom.

Ten

Those butterflies in Nora's stomach took flight all at once and swirled in circles.

Mouth dry, nerves strained to the aching point, she clung to Mike as he moved quickly through the dark house. Outside his bedroom, he stopped, reached for the knob and threw the door open with so much force it smacked against the wall behind it. He stepped into the room and his arms tightened around her.

Moonlight slanted into the room through the uncurtained window and spread across the wide bed, extending a pale invitation. The handmade quilt covering the mattress looked soft, welcoming. He carried her to the bed and stopped alongside it. Looking down at her, he again asked, ''You're sure about this?''

Nora slid the flat of her hand down his chest and tweaked open one of his shirt buttons. ''I told you. I'm sure. Not a doubt in my mind. Uh-huh, this is what I want. Right now. You. Here. With me. On that bed. I mean it—''

He grinned and Nora's heart did a wild, staggering dance.

''I get it,'' he said, and, still holding her, bent down and reached with one hand to throw the quilt to the foot of the bed. ''You're sure.''

''Oh, yeah.''

''Good,'' he muttered, and knelt on the bed so he could stretch her out across the mattress. '''Cause I'm not sure I could take it if you changed your mind now.''

''No problem there,'' she told him. Her butterflies had butterflies. Every inch of her skin felt alive. Sizzling. One look from him and she felt the fire inside her erupt into a volcano of pulsing need and hunger that she'd never expected to be so strong. And soon, very soon, she'd be leaving virginity behind. She'd take the step she'd been waiting so long for. And best of all, it would be Mike showing her the secret hand-shake.

His hand swept beneath the hem of her impossibly

expensive nightie and caressed her bare skin and…

"My purse!"

"What?" His fingers stilled on her abdomen.

"I need my purse. I left it in the kitchen—"

"Going somewhere?" he asked lazily, dragging his fingertips across her belly.

She sucked in air, blew it out and shivered as she said, "No. It's just—I didn't want to buy them in Te-soro, because you know this town, and everyone would be talking and they'd all figure out what I was doing…I mean what we were doing, so I stopped at a store in Monterey this afternoon and picked up—"

"You're babbling," he pointed out, and she heard the smile in his voice.

"I'm lucky I can talk," she said, and sucked at air again as his fingertips danced along the edges of her panties.

"Then don't," he said, dipping his head to take her mouth with a series of brief, tantalizing, nibbling kisses. "Don't talk. Just feel. Just—"

"Oh, I like that," she whispered, and wondered if he heard her over the roar of her heartbeat.

"Good," he said, "so do I."

Another nibble. Another taste. Another too quick kiss that left her hungry, frantic, for more.

His mouth dipped to the line of her jaw and down her throat. She felt his lips, his teeth, his tongue, draw-ing a line of fire across her skin. Her brain blurred.

She'd needed to tell him something. Started to tell him about the store...*oh, my*...and that she had some...*wow*... Air. She needed air. Silently, Nora reminded herself to breathe, but there was just so much more going on in her brain right now, she was afraid that order was going to come in low on her list of priorities.

"So soft," he murmured, and his breath dusted warmth against her skin.

"Mike..." *Think,* she told herself. "In my purse..."

He rose up, looked down at her and smiled. "What could possibly be so important about your purse?"

Her eyes were rolling. That was the only explanation for the fact that his face looked blurry. She inhaled sharply, deeply, and focused. When she found her voice again, she managed to say, "Condoms. There're condoms in my purse."

That slow smile of his deepened as he shook his head. "You're amazing, you know that?"

A flutter of something delicious wafted through her. "Because I can shop?"

"Yeah," he murmured, letting his gaze slide over her and following that trail with his fingertips. He barely touched her, caressing her so gently it was as if a feather was dancing across her skin. Tendrils of expectation unwound throughout her body. Her blood went to a slow simmer and a deep, throbbing ache settled low in her body, making Nora want to twitch and writhe beneath him.

Her eager responses fed Mike's hunger until he could barely see her through the haze of want and need that nearly blinded him. His heart crashed against his rib cage and breathing was damn near impossible. He felt tight and hard and ready to roll. But he had to control his own desires. Had to slow things down. Had to make sure he took his time.

It'd been years since he'd been with a virgin. And hell, he'd been a virgin himself then. But he'd learned plenty over the years and he was determined to see to it that Nora's first time was a hell of a lot more memorable than his had been.

The condoms could wait, though he was grateful she'd thought of them. Especially since he didn't have his own stash. He hadn't exactly been a social animal the last couple of years.

But none of that mattered now. The only thing on his mind was Nora. How best to show her everything. How to take her high enough that she wouldn't mind the fall.

Skimming his hands beneath the hem of that incredible nightie, Mike relished the feel of her soft, smooth skin beneath his palms. Her curves were generous, and he followed every line until he knew her body by touch and she was squirming beneath him.

''I want to touch you, too,'' she said, and Mike had to smile.

He wanted her hands on him as much as she did, so he stood up and quickly stripped, tearing his clothes and boots off and tossing them into a corner of the room. He watched her watching him and saw her eyes widen.

When he lay down beside her again, she reached up and ran her hands across his chest, skimming her fingers through the short, dark hair and dragging her nails against his skin until he was pretty sure she'd branded him. He gritted his teeth, pulled in air like a drowning man and fought for control. It was a hard-won battle.

Finally, when he couldn't take another second of her gentle torture, he took her hands in one of his and pinned them behind her head on the mattress. She arched her back and her breasts pushed against their lace prison. Her nipples peaked and Mike's mouth watered.

Using his free hand, he pushed the hem of her nightie high until her breasts lay bare in the moonlight. Nora twisted slightly, moving into him, and her breath came in short, hard gasps. She trembled, and he felt the shudder of her movement move through him as well, touching the dark and lonely heart of him.

He dipped his head.

She held her breath.

He took first one nipple, then the next into his

mouth and Nora groaned aloud, arching into him, pushing herself at him as if afraid he would stop. But there was no chance of that.

"Perfect," he murmured, and ran the tip of his tongue across the dark pink, rigid tip of her breast.

"Mike...oh my...Mike..."

He smiled against her flesh. So Nora, to keep talking. He tasted her again, pulling her nipple deep into his mouth, suckling her, teasing her with the edges of his teeth, driving her into a frenzy of need that had her bucking beneath him in a futile attempt to ease the ache within.

"So good," she said brokenly. "It feels so...good. So...right."

His own body tightened as she moved into him again and again, seeking something she'd never known before. He felt her frustration and shared it. He wanted to be inside her, pushing himself home, deep into her warmth. He wanted to claim her for his own.

"Mike...I need—I need—"

"I know, honey," he whispered, lifting his mouth just long enough to shift and taste her other breast. She rocked and moved beneath him again. She tried to pull her hands free of his grip, but Mike held her tighter. He didn't want her touching him now. If she did, he'd lose all semblance of control.

While he tasted her breasts, he slid his free hand down the length of her body. Hooking his fingers beneath the edge of her panties, he pushed them down, over her hips, and as she lifted herself off the bed, he scooped them down and off her legs. Then slowly, teasingly, he ran his hand up the length of her leg, up her calf, past her knee and up along the inside of her thigh. His fingertips blazed a trail of heat and need and she responded eagerly, frantically.

Twisting her head from side to side on the bed, she swallowed hard, licked her lips and gave up trying to escape Mike's strong grip on her wrists.

"Please," she whispered, her voice carrying an ache that echoed inside him. "Please, I need…"

"This," he said, rising up to look into her eyes. His fingertips found her center, damp and hot and ready. Her body jerked at his first intimate touch and a shuddering groan slipped past her throat.

"Oh, Mike…"

"Just feel it, honey," he urged, bending his head to kiss her mouth, her cheeks. "Let it come, then let go and enjoy the ride."

"But…I…can't…breathe…."

A slow grin teased the corner of his mouth. "For this, you don't need air."

Her eyes flashed from blue to smoky-gray as she twisted beneath him. Planting her feet on the mattress, she lifted her hips, welcoming him deeper, faster.

Nora forgot about trying to breathe. All she wanted to think about was what was happening to other parts of her body. She'd never known this wild, frenzied sense of anticipation. Nothing in her life had prepared her for the sheer, raw power of sex. Her brain blurred. Thoughts whisked in and out of her mind so quickly she couldn't have caught one if she'd been trying.

His fingers, magical fingers, touched her, dipping into her body with a maniacal rhythm that pulsed and pounded deep within her. His thumb brushed against a single, unbelievably sensitive spot and Nora nearly screamed. Or would have, if she'd had enough air.

Mike was everything.

His touch.

His kiss.

His body, pressed to hers.

He pushed her higher and higher, and when she thought she'd reached her limit, he pushed her over the edge and her body erupted into a startling burst of sensation that rippled and poured through her in a stream of pleasure so deep, so wide, her only choice was to sink into it and drown.

"I'll be right back," he whispered huskily close to her ear.

Nora couldn't move. Couldn't see. Oh. Open your eyes, Nora. She did and stared blindly up at the ceiling. It was spinning. No, *she* was spinning.

"Mike?" She was pretty sure she said it out loud. But her hearing seemed to be gone, too.

"I'm here," he said a second later, and she felt him join her on the bed.

"Where'd you go?"

"To get your purse."

Her eyes widened and she turned her head to look at him. One dark eyebrow arched and his mouth was curved into that half grin she'd come to love. Instantly, her body went on full alert again. She wouldn't have believed it possible, but she was ready for more.

"I want you inside me, Mike," she said, and watched his features tighten. "I want to feel you within me."

He pushed one hand through her hair, scooping it back from her face, and his thumb traced a slow pattern on her temple. "You're killin' me, Nora."

She smiled. "Oh, not yet."

He grinned again. "Not through with me, then?"

"Not a chance, cowboy," she promised, and rolled onto her side so she could wrap her arms around his neck and pull his head to hers for a kiss. She slanted her mouth over his and slid her tongue past his parted lips. She took his breath and was grateful for it. She smoothed her hands over his bare back, loving the feel of his hard, muscled flesh. She pressed her body close, smashing her breasts against his chest, and then moved, rubbing her sensitized nipples until spirals of newly awakened need erupted inside her.

Mike took all she had and then offered it back to

her. His hands moved over her body, defining every curve, exploring every valley. He couldn't touch her enough. Couldn't feel enough of her silky, flower scented skin. And when neither of them could wait another moment, he pulled away from her long enough to snatch up one of the condoms she'd brought with her and put it on.

Then he laid her back against the mattress and knelt between her upraised thighs, spread open for him. He looked down at her and touched her gently, gingerly, and felt her tremble from head to foot.

He moved then, covering her body with his, pushing himself into her damp heat, claiming her as she wanted to be claimed.

Nora dug her fingers into his shoulders and held on as she stared up into his forest-green eyes. She felt him take her. Inch by glorious inch. Slowly, deliberately, he moved deeper, closer. She rocked her hips, trying to accommodate him, trying to ease his passage, trying to ease the ache building all over again inside her.

Then he paused for a moment and in one smooth, long stroke entered her fully, completely. A quick flash of pain rose up and was gone again. Nora winced, then shifted her hips and relished the amazing sensation of actually being joined with Mike. Having him a part of her. Locked together.

"You okay?"

"I'm way better than okay," she managed to say around the knot lodged in her throat.

Lifting herself up from the bed, she kissed him. And when he followed her back down, she gave him everything she had to give. His hips set a rhythm that was fast and sure and solid. She moved with him, aching to feel that explosion of power within her again. This time, as it built and roared to a crest inside her, she knew what was coming and didn't fight it. Didn't fear it. Didn't hold back.

She opened herself to the feelings. To him. This was what she'd been waiting for. This magic. This wonder. Electricity hummed through her veins. Anticipation swelled inside her. She held her breath when the first tremor shook her soul, then screamed as it tore through her with a wildness she hadn't known existed.

"Mike!" She yelled his name, and her voice seemed to echo in the moonlit room.

"Come with me," he murmured, levering himself up on one elbow so he could catch her gaze with his. "Come with me, Nora. Fly."

"Take me with you," she said on a sigh that dissolved into a moan.

He took her higher still, and when he felt her body's surrender, he gave himself up to the release that had been building for weeks. He shouted her name into the moonlight, and together they fell into the heart of the storm.

Eleven

———

"**W**ow." Nora's voice sounded froggy even to her. But she was pretty impressed with herself that she'd managed to get that word out, anyway. Of course, it didn't come close to describing what she was feeling.

"Same to you," Mike whispered, and rolled to one side of her before lying there gasping for air like a dying man.

Nora stared up at the ceiling and waited until the overhead beams stopped swimming before she spoke again. "I realize," she said, "that I have no frame of reference. But I think that was pretty good."

He laughed shortly. "Yeah, I'd say so."

"Oh, man, I never thought I'd hear myself ask this. I sound like some dumb old movie, but I just can't help myself, because I really want to know and how will I know if I don't ask, so it's not really dumb if you think about it and—"

Mike held up one hand. "Nora, what?"

"Was it good for you?"

He shot her a look that told her plainly he thought she was nuts to have to ask. And that one incredulous stare did more for her than anything he could say. Still, it was nice to hear the words.

"It was…great." He kept staring at her as if seeing her for the first time. "Amazing."

He reached out and skimmed one hand down the length of her body and Nora's skin tingled expectantly. Her breath caught and a now-familiar aching want began to grow deep within her. "Oh, boy," she whispered, and moved beneath his touch, silently encouraging him.

Mike smiled knowingly. "What is it?"

Nora gulped in air, then blew it out again. "I just had no idea I could go from vestal virgin to wanton woman in the space of an hour."

"Wonton woman?"

She laughed. "Not wonton. *Wanton.* And I know that's a word."

"Is it ever?" he groaned as he pulled her close and then maneuvered her until she was lying on top of him. Stretched out, skin to skin, heartbeat to heartbeat. His hands skimmed down her back and over the curve of her bottom.

Nora closed her eyes as his fingers kneaded her tender flesh. Beneath her, she felt his body stirring to life again. Instantly, she flushed with a rush of heat so powerful, she was pretty sure the ends of her hair were singed. "Whoa."

"'Whoa' as in stop?" he teased.

She took his face between her palms, and looking him square in the eye, she said softly, "Don't you dare." Then she bent her head and kissed him. Mouths melded, tongues explored and twisted together, joined in a dance designed to stir bodies into life. Nora moved atop him, straddling him, and as their kiss deepened, she slid her hands down, across his chest, loving the feel of his hard, strong body.

Loving.

She loved the way he touched her. She loved the sound of his voice. His booming laugh. She loved his tenderness with Emily. The strength he'd shown in rebuilding his life. She loved his sense of humor and his sense of responsibility.

She loved him.

That thought hit her with a startling blast of clarity just as his hands swept down her body to once again explore her intimately. Breaking their kiss, she went up on her knees and watched him watching her. She saw his green eyes darken with desire, passion, and her breath caught at the rush of female power that swept through her.

She wiggled her hips and saw him gasp, closing his eyes as if praying for strength. But his hope went unanswered as she moved again, deliberately lifting her hips high enough to take his body into hers again. Slowly, proudly, she lowered herself onto his length, taking him deep within her. He filled her, reaching into the dark, empty parts of her heart and soul that she'd once feared would always be left wanting.

Her breasts ached for his touch. Her heart ached to hear words he wasn't willing to say.

Nora moved in a slow, rocking motion that set off sparklers of pleasure inside her. She felt the glorious bursts of sensation exploding inside, and even while her brain focused on the pleasure, she tried to memorize it all, to put it down in stone somewhere in her brain. Because she never wanted to forget this moment. The moment when she'd realized her love for Mike and celebrated that love by taking him deeper inside her than she'd ever believed possible.

Mike's hands swept up and down her body. Tweaking her nipples until she arched into his touch, demanding more. In the bright moonlight, her hair shone like silver, her skin gleamed like porcelain, and when she moved on him again, she looked like some otherworldly goddess. His blood boiled, his body ached and his brain shut down. All he could think about was touching her, feeling her, tasting her. He wanted her flat on her back and under him. He wanted to part her legs and taste her secrets. He wanted it all. And he wanted it with Nora.

He'd thought that tonight, he would be the teacher. But instead, she'd taught him just how much he still had to learn. He'd never felt this way before. Never experienced this…connection with any other woman. And now was not the time to try to make sense of it.

Dropping one hand to the spot where their bodies joined, he rubbed her most sensitive spot with a delicate touch that nearly sent her through the ceiling. Her body tightened around him, squeezing him hard and sure in a warm, velvety grip.

And when he couldn't take it another minute, he flipped her onto her back and stared down into her wide, surprised eyes.

"Mike—"

"Nora," he said with a tense smile, "do us both a favor and be quiet."

"Right," she said, and lifted her legs to lock them around his hips. She pulled him against her, moving with his rocking hips, holding on to him, digging her short nails into his back. He felt it all, relished it all. And when the first tremor started inside her, he gave himself up to the same wonder and, with one long thrust, pushed them both over the edge into oblivion.

* * *

An hour or two later…who could be sure?—Nora stumbled from the bedroom into the kitchen. She needed water. And maybe food. She'd never felt so energized and so tired and so…sore in her life. Sex was probably the best exercise in the world. She wondered why no one ever mentioned *that* in all of those videos and books.

She shivered and pulled the edges of Mike's tattered terry-cloth robe tighter around her waist. She'd found the worn black thing hanging on a hook in the master bathroom, and since Mike was still snoozing, she'd helped herself. Nora stubbed her toe as she crossed the hall and did a little half dance as she waited for her toe to stop aching.

"Serves you right for not leaving another light on," she muttered as she rounded a corner into the still brightly lit kitchen. She headed right for the refrigerator and pulled the door open. It was pretty well stocked, considering a man did all the shopping. *And what a man,* she thought as she reached for a fried chicken leg and a bottle of water.

Shutting the refrigerator, she carried her prize to the kitchen table and sat down. She reached for a napkin, then uncapped the bottle of water and took a long, satisfying drink. Her body was still humming and her brain was still trying to decide what to do about the whole "I love Mike" situation when the back door flew open.

Hand at her throat, Nora jumped to her feet just as Rick shouted, "Mike!"

"Oh, my…" Nora's voice trailed off into an embarrassed silence. Not only was she naked under Mike's robe, but the robe was ratty and threadbare and—oh, for heaven's sake. Did it really matter how tacky the robe was?

An instant later, he noticed her. Snatching his hat off, Rick looked her up and down and then quickly ducked his head and shifted his gaze to anywhere but at her. "Sorry, Nora. I uh…didn't know you were here and I…"

Why was *he* embarrassed? At least *he* was dressed!

"What the hell's all the shouting about?" Mike grumbled as he rushed into the kitchen. Bare-chested, he'd taken the time to pull on a pair of jeans, but they were unbuttoned and he was barefoot. His dark hair was ruffled from Nora's crazed fingers and he looked…well, she thought, he looked like he'd just been doing a happy dance on *her*.

Could this get any better?

Rick looked at Mike and scraped one hand over his face. "I'm sorry about interrupting you and—look, I just wanted to tell you that Donna's in labor and we're headed to the hospital. Probably won't be here in the morning."

Mike's gaze shifted from Rick to Nora and back again. Slapping the other man on the back, he said,

"That's great, Rick. Give Donna a good-luck kiss from me."

"I will." Rick deliberately kept his gaze from Nora as he turned and headed back to the door. Before he stepped outside, he said, "'Night, Nora."

Once the back door was closed and they were alone again, Nora glanced at him. "Well, that was fun."

A smile twitched at the corner of his mouth. "You know, even if he hadn't seen you tonight, he would have spotted your car first thing in the morning. He'd have known you spent the night."

"Yeah," she admitted. "But he wouldn't have a mental photo of me in your robe." She ran her fingers down what used to be a lapel. "And speaking of robes, cowboy…you really ought to splurge and buy a new one."

"Why?" he asked, and moved toward her slowly. "From where I'm standing, it looks pretty good."

"Really?"

"Oh, yeah," he assured her. When he stopped directly in front of her, his hands dropped to the knotted belt at her waist. Tugging it open, he pushed the edges of the robe wide and cupped her breasts in his palms.

"Oh, my," Nora sighed, and leaned into him, loving the feel of his fingers on her nipples. The light, teasing touch. The gentle pull and tug on her flesh that brought a wild response to completely unrelated parts of her body.

"You were hungry, huh?" he asked, glancing at the now-forgotten chicken leg on the table.

"Mmm-hmm…"

"Me, too," he murmured, and before she could wonder what he was up to, he'd picked her up and plopped her down on the edge of the table.

"Mike…" Nora's heart rate quickened until she thought it just might leap from her throat—and then where would she be? As he dropped to his knees in front of her, she fought for breath. *What was he…?* She fought for strength. Fought to keep from reaching for him. "Mike, what're you—"

"I told you," he said, and gently parted her thighs, "I just want a little snack."

She gasped as he bent and took her with his mouth. Incredible sensations pooled at her center and then sent long, winding ribbons of need spooling throughout her body. Air staggered in and out of her lungs. She couldn't look away. She watched him as he gave her the most intimate of kisses. She saw him taste her, savor her, and felt herself dissolve in a fresh explosion of desire.

Nora clutched at the edge of the old oak pedestal table. She rocked into him and nearly fell over when she felt his tongue slide across her flesh and dip into the heart of her. Too much, she thought. Too much and not nearly enough. *Never stop,* she silently pleaded. She moaned frantically as he lifted her legs and rested them on his shoulders. His arms came around her bottom and held her firmly in place while his mouth took her places she'd never dreamed existed.

And this time, when she shattered, she wasn't thinking clearly enough to keep her mouth shut. This time when she shouted his name, it changed everything.

"Mike…" she called out, "I love you."

A few minutes later, the words were still hanging in the air like a neon sign. They couldn't be ignored. Mike helped her down from the table, then turned and walked across the room, trying to think of something to say that wouldn't hurt her. But there wasn't a thing he could do to ease this.

"Nora," he said as he trained his gaze on one of the windows and the darkened yard beyond. "I told you before—I'm not the man you need."

He heard her approach, her bare feet making almost no sound on the linoleum. She stood behind him, and he saw her reflection in the window glass. Her eyes looked overly bright and he prayed desperately that it wasn't the gleam of tears he was seeing.

Damn it. He'd blown it good this time. He never should have given into the desire swamping him. He should have sent her home when she showed up in his kitchen looking like every man's fantasy. But to do that he would have had to be a saint. And God knew he was no saint.

She put her hand on his arm, and the warmth of her fingers seemed to spear deeply inside him. It had been so long since he'd felt…anything…that having her touch him so completely was a danger that rocked him even as it enticed him.

"Relax, Mike," she said, smiling, and leaned her forehead against his bare shoulder. "I didn't propose."

"I don't want to hurt you, Nora," he said tightly, and knew he was about to do just that. "But you're making too much of this. It was sex. Great sex, but sex. Desire. Not love."

She didn't say anything, so he kept talking. For the first time in three weeks, she was being quiet. And that pretty much unnerved him. Turning around to face her, he forced himself to look down into her eyes. No tears. Good. "You're a virgin and—"

"*Was* a virgin," she interrupted.

"Exactly. You're emotional. I mean, I'm your first, so you're making more of this than there is."

Nora straightened the robe and tightened the belt around her waist. It couldn't have been easy for a woman to look regal in his worn-out bathrobe. But she managed.

"Don't start treating me like I'm an idiot, Mike, or I'm really going to get mad."

That he didn't need. "Fine. The point is, I like you, Nora. Hell, I'm real fond of you."

"Gee, be still my heart. Oh. Wait a minute. It is."

He ignored the sarcasm and tried again. "You're a hell of a woman, Nora. I admire you a lot. I like spending time with you." He cupped her shoulders and held her in a firm grip that kept him somehow from pulling her close and wrapping his arms around her. "But love's just not in the picture."

Nora looked up at him, saw the regret in his eyes and felt something inside her shatter. Disappointment welled up, sure and strong. For some stupid reason, she'd thought that once she'd said the words, he'd be able to admit that there was more here than desire. But, clearly, he was determined to ignore the very real hum of electricity arcing between them.

Well, fine. But she wouldn't have him feeling sorry for her. She didn't want his sympathy. She wanted his love. And if she couldn't get that, then she wouldn't let him know that it hurt. Sure, she usually believed in honesty. But sometimes even the most honest person had to lie.

Pulling in a deep breath, she blew it out again, met his gaze and told the biggest whopper of her life. "It's okay, Mike. It's not like I want anything from you." She reached up and laid one hand on his cheek. Her heart ached, but her voice was clear. "I love you, but I'll get over it."

He blinked, flinched and shifted position uneasily. Strangely enough, that made her feel better. So she went with it.

"Really. I mean, you were a big help. Now that I'm not a virgin anymore, I'm sure I'll be able to find someone else."

Did his eyes narrow, or was that wishful thinking?

She rose up on her toes and gave him a brief, hard kiss that practically burned her mouth. "I'm sure that once I get into the 'swinging single' life, I'll get over you." Oh, boy, lying was becoming easier. That couldn't be a good sign.

Nora was amazed that he was buying this. Did he really believe that she could respond to him the way she had and then go to someone else? She'd never forget his touch. Never forget the magic she'd found in his arms. And she couldn't even imagine letting anyone else touch her.

But he didn't need to know that, did he?

"Swinging single?" he asked tightly, and a muscle in his jaw twitched.

"You know what I mean," she said, and ran one hand through her hair as she kept talking. "I mean, we both knew this was temporary, and I guess I'll have to find my own man after this, because it's probably not a good idea for you and me to keep spending time together and—"

"You're babbling," he growled, and pulled her close.

Pressed flat against him, she gloried in the hard, solid strength of him and hoped desperately it wouldn't be for the last time.

His gaze moved over her features. "If things were different—"

"Things are different," she pointed out. "I'm not Vicky."

"I know that," he snapped. "But I thought that would work out, too, and it didn't. I can't risk Emily's happiness."

Damn his ex-wife, Nora thought. The woman was gone, but her legacy lingered. She'd burned Mike so thoroughly he was willing to lock his heart away forever rather than take a chance.

"I'm not asking you to."

"You're asking for something."

Yes, she was. She was asking for his heart, but he wasn't ready or willing to give it. So she settled for one more piece of magic. "Another kiss?" she said. "One for the road?"

"Nora—"

"Shut up, cowboy, and kiss me."

His mouth came down on hers and she gave herself over to the joy of the moment. And when he carried her back down the hall to the bedroom, she tried not to think about the fact that it was probably for the last time.

All night, they came together in a wild tangle of desire and need, and in the morning, when Mike woke up, Nora was gone.

He was alone.

Nora buried herself in pastries.

Well, baking them, anyway.

For the first time in her life, she wasn't hungry. The next few days stumbled along, one after the other, and she told herself that it would get easier. All she had to do was forget Mike.

No problem.

Shouldn't be any more difficult than, say, forgetting how to breathe.

The shop kept her busy during the day, but at night, alone in her house, she felt surrounded by memories. Her body burned for Mike's touch and she caught herself straining to hear the sound of his truck coming down the street. She thought about calling him, but she drew the line at being that pathetic.

She wouldn't become a whiny, needy female. She'd survived twenty-eight years without a man and she could do it again. "Although," she muttered as she pulled yet another pan of cinnamon rolls from the oven, "it's easy enough to live without something you never had. But once you've had it, you kind of miss it."

"Talking to yourself again?"

She shot a glance at the swinging door and gave Molly a half smile as she stepped into the kitchen.

"Hi."

"Wow. Now, there's a greeting designed to make a person feel all warm and toasty."

"You want warm toast?" Nora asked, and pointed to another tray. "There you go."

Molly shook her head, grabbed a chair and dragged it over to the counter where Nora was busy slicing a log of cookie dough. "Criminy it's hot in here." She tugged at the scoop neck of her tank top.

"Oven," Nora said shortly. Her own tank top and shorts helped beat the heat inside the bakery, but in some ways, she found the heat comforting.

"You've been in hiding," her friend accused.

"Not hiding," Nora told her. "Just working."

"You didn't let me know how it went with Mike the other night."

Nora lifted her gaze to her friend's.

"Ah," Molly said sympathetically. "Not so good."

"Actually, it was—" Nora paused, holding the knife's edge on the dough "—amazing."

"Congrats. The deed is done."

"Well and completely done," Nora said. "Several times."

"Wow." Envy colored Molly's voice.

"Everything was great." She sighed. "Until I told him I loved him."

"Ouch."

"That about sums it up."

Being a true and loyal friend, Molly said the perfect thing. "He's an idiot."

"Agreed," Nora said, and finished her slicing. Then, picking up the slices, she spread them on a cookie sheet with practiced ease. "But he's *my* idiot."

"Uh-huh," Molly said, and reached for one of the still-hot cinnamon rolls. "So, what are you doing about it?"

"I'm letting him miss me."

"Is it working?"

"I miss *him*," she said. "Does that count?"

Molly pulled off a small piece of the pastry, popped it in her mouth and said thoughtfully, "My guess is, if you're missing him, then he's missing you."

Small consolation, she thought as she turned and slid the cookie tray into the oven. He wasn't missing her enough to come to town. She hadn't seen him or Emily in the last three days.

Nora straightened up, turned around and looked at her friend. "Love's not for sissies, is it?"

Molly shook her head. "Nope. But it's worth it, if you hang in there."

"I don't know, Moll." Nora took a seat opposite

the other woman. Bracing her elbows on the marble counter, she let the coolness slip into her skin and hoped it would chill the fires still burning inside her. "I finally found love—with the one man who doesn't want me."

A hard thing to admit. Her sisters were furious at Mike, her mother was reading the singles ads again and her customers were whispering whenever she walked into the front room. Everyone in Tesoro was talking about her and Mike.

And she didn't care. All she knew was that her business wasn't as much fun if she couldn't tell Mike about her day. Her afternoons dragged on forever because she couldn't go to the ranch to help Mike exercise his horses. Her evenings were empty because she wasn't reading bedtime stories to Emily, tucking her in or getting good-night kisses.

But the nights were the worst. Alone in the dark, she relived that one night with Mike. She recalled every kiss, every touch. What it felt like to stretch out her hand to find him right there. She remembered his heartbeat in the night, his arms closing around her and his body sliding into hers.

Molly suddenly blurred and Nora blinked away the tears welling in her eyes.

"He makes me so mad, Moll," Nora said sadly. "We could have had everything, if he'd just been willing to risk his heart."

Twelve

The longest three days of Mike's life crawled past at a snail's pace.

His mood was black as sin, and anyone with half a brain would have steered clear. But Rick, still flying high from the birth of his son, was apparently oblivious to the warning signs.

"I'm tellin' you, Mike, that boy of mine can eat his weight in formula."

"Swell." Mike concentrated on the fence post, putting his shoulder against it and leaning. The damn thing had to come out before he could replace it—and it looked as though he would be doing all the work around here himself today. He glanced at Rick. The other man was leaning against the truck fender, ankles crossed, arms folded over his chest and a stupid smile on his face.

Funny. Mike had never really noticed just how irritating someone else's happiness could be.

"Donna did a great job," Rick was saying, his voice wistful as he strolled down memory lane. "You should have seen her. No tears. No screams. Some woman down the hall was shouting loud enough to bring down the hospital."

Mike winced. He remembered Emily's birth clearly, too. Vicky had been that woman screaming. She'd called him every name in the book and then some. She'd screamed at the nurses and the doctors and then hadn't even been interested in her child when she was finally born.

Maybe it would have been better for Vicky if their "accidental" pregnancy hadn't happened. But he'd never regret Emily. And, in a way, Emily's birth had cleared the air with Vicky, too. The woman had shown her true colors and then done him the favor of disappearing from his life.

And he and his daughter had been just fine on their own. Until Nora. Mike's mind instantly conjured her laughing image and he gritted his teeth in response. Damn it. He'd been happy. Well, content, at least. And then she'd come along and made him look forward to seeing her. Hearing her.

She'd brought flowers into his house and light into his heart. And damn it…he hadn't *asked* her to.

"Donna was just amazing," Rick was repeating, still awed by the whole miracle of his son's birth.

Caught by the wonder in the other man's voice, Mike found himself imagining what it might have been like if Nora had been Emily's mother. He couldn't picture Nora screaming and cursing at him. He couldn't even pretend to imagine Nora turning away from her child.

He stopped in his efforts to dislodge the fence post and let his mind wander further. He saw images of Nora, pregnant with his child. Nora holding Emily's hand and laughing. The three of them sitting at the kitchen table at dinner. And then his brain picked up speed and apparently decided that if torturing him was the object of this little fantasy, then it ought to do it right.

As clear as day, he saw four or five kids, running wild on the ranch. He saw Nora and him sitting on the porch in the evening, with her on his lap as they laughed at the kids playing with a litter of puppies. In his mind, the old house was lit up like a Christmas tree and the sounds of laughter surrounded it like a protective halo.

Then just as quickly as it came, the vision ended

and he was back in the field, straining against a fence post, listening to Rick ramble. His temper suddenly flared, sharp and hot, and he glared at the other man.

"You gonna help me with this or just stand there holding up that truck all day?"

"Sorry." Rick jumped away from the truck, took up a position on the other side of the fence post and started shoving. But while he worked, Rick decided to take his life in his hands. "Haven't seen Nora in a while," he said. "Everything all right?"

Mike shot him a look that should have fried him. "Everything's just dandy. Can we work now?"

"Yes, sir, boss." Rick ducked his head, but not before Mike saw the flash of annoyance in his friend's eyes.

Great. Now not only was he without Nora, but if this kept up he wouldn't have any friends left, either. Oh, yeah, this was working out fine.

"These cookies are yucky," Emily complained, and dropped her half-eaten chocolate chip cookie back into the bag sitting on the front seat of the truck.

"They're your favorite," Mike argued.

"Nora's are better."

Yeah, they were, he silently agreed. He'd taken Emily to a bakery in Monterey, but it just wasn't the same. It had been five days now since he'd seen Nora and Mike was busy convincing himself that it was for the best. To help himself, he'd been avoiding her like the plague. But it just wasn't any good. He could keep from seeing her, but her presence continued to be felt. She'd infiltrated every corner of his world.

Her love for his daughter.

The paintings she'd done with Emily.

Hell, her scent was still lingering in his bedroom.

"Nora says she's gonna help me make a costume for the spring play."

"What?" Mike shifted his brain back into gear and focused on his daughter.

Emily sighed dramatically and gave him one of those patient looks that he swore females were born knowing how to deliver.

"Nora says she's gonna help me—"

"Yeah, I heard that part," he said, wanting to catch his favorite little girl before she launched into a long, detailed explanation. "When did you see Nora?"

"Yesterday," she said, and licked chocolate off her fingertips.

"Yesterday?"

"Uh-huh."

Scowling, Mike asked, "Where did you see her?"

"At school. She comes and has lunch with me."

Nora went to Emily's school? "How long's she been doing this?"

"A *really* long time," Emily said, as if she and

Nora had been doing lunch for centuries. "I like Nora.
She's nice, Daddy."

Mike just stared at his daughter for a minute. How
long had Nora been meeting Emily at school for
lunch? Why had no one told *him?* And why was Nora
still going to the school? Their little bargain was finished. She was no longer a virgin, so the very reason
they'd been spending time together was finished. Nora
hadn't been to the ranch in five long days. He'd been
avoiding her and he was pretty sure she'd been doing
the same. But, apparently, she hadn't cut her ties to
Emily.

Something warm and bright and a lot like hope rose
up inside him. At the same time, he had to face the
realization that he'd been a class A jerk. He'd cut Nora
off at the knees. Turned his back on what had happened between them because he'd convinced himself
it was the only way to protect Emily. But Nora, it
seemed, had her own way of taking care of the child.
And that involved maintaining ties that Mike had been
so intent on cutting.

"Daddy," the little girl beside him asked in a voice
filled with confusion, "how come Nora doesn't come
out to the ranch anymore?"

Hmm. How to answer that one? The truth? Obviously not. After all, he couldn't very well admit to his
only child that she had an idiot for a father. So what
could he say?

"Well, Nora's really busy and—"

"Did you ask her to stay with us?" Emily interrupted, and gave him a look that demanded an answer.

"No, honey," he said. "I didn't."

"How come?" she asked, and wiped her mouth, dragging a line of chocolate from her lips halfway up her cheek.

Good question. How come, indeed?

"People won't stay if you don't ask 'em to," she pointed out with all the sweet wisdom of a child.

"I guess you're right," he said. If he had taken Nora's declaration of love and returned it, would she have stayed? Would she have taken a chance on him and a ready-made family?

Hell, he knew the answer to that question without even thinking about it. Of course she would. Nora wasn't Vicky. Nora was funny and smart and kind and she already loved Emily as if she were her own child. And she'd shown *him* more love in the last several weeks than he'd known in years.

A knot formed in the pit of his stomach, and he had to grit his teeth to keep from spitting at himself in disgust. He'd blown it. Big time. He'd been so busy protecting himself and using Emily as an excuse for hiding from the world that he'd missed his chance at *real* love. The happily-ever-after kind.

And he had only himself to blame for it.

Damn it, he'd lost at love before and been burned badly enough to convince him to avoid it. But it had found him again, anyway—he'd just been too damn scared to risk it. And this time, the pain of losing what he might have had was so much worse. Because what he felt for Nora was so much bigger and deeper than anything he'd ever known before.

Grumbling under his breath, he fired up the engine. "Fasten your seat belt, Em," he said.

"Are we gonna go see Nora?" she asked hopefully, and snapped the strap into the buckle.

"Nope," he said, and watched her face fall. Reaching over, he tipped her chin up with the tips of his fingers and smiled at her. "*You're* going home. *I'm* going to see Nora." Some things you just had to do on your own. Though he thought he might stand a better chance of winning Nora over if Emily was with him, Mike discarded the notion. He wanted her to take *him*. Not just his child. He knew she loved Emily.

Now he had to know if she still *loved* him enough to give him a second chance.

"Are you gonna ask her to stay with us, Daddy?"

Ask.

Beg.

Argue.

Whatever it took, he told himself, and steered the truck into traffic.

* * *

Nora looked around at her customers, then shifted her gaze to the wide front window that opened onto Main street. Spring sunshine sprinkled the ground like a promise of coming summer.

The crowds were thick, business was brisk, and all Nora wanted to do was close up shop and head out to the ranch. She leaned her elbows on the counter and brought up the image of her watching Mike working on his horses. If she tried, she could almost feel the sun on her face and hear the wind brushing through the trees. Imaginary Mike turned and gave her a blinding smile that sent bolts of heat shooting through her bloodstream.

"Well, hi Nora," a deep voice murmured from close by.

She jerked out of her lovely daydream to face Bill Hammond. His interested brown gaze swept over her quickly and thoroughly, and Nora felt the sudden urge to cross her arms over her breasts.

"Hi, Bill. What can I get for you?" She nearly winced at the simple question she asked daily.

"Well, now," Bill said as he leaned over the top of the glass display case and gave her a look she was willing to bet he considered one of his best *"Hello Baby"* come-ons.

"I can think of quite a few things that you could get for me."

Nora plastered a polite smile on her face but inwardly hurried him along. Her heart just wasn't in the flirting mood anymore.

Mike stood outside the bakery and rehearsed for the tenth time in the last fifteen minutes exactly what he wanted to say to Nora. That was assuming she'd be in the mood to listen to him at all.

Finally, he decided to just go with his gut. He reached for the doorknob. That's when he spotted Bill leaning in toward Nora and leering at her. A string of warning bells went off in Mike's mind. If he didn't fight for what he wanted *now,* then he'd spend the rest of his life regretting it. Mike watched Bill trying to make one of his patented moves, and in response, frustration and anger bubbled together inside him.

This was his future. If he couldn't convince Nora that he did love her, then he was going to be sentenced to seeing her with some other guy. A guy who would have the right to hold her, love her. A guy who would hear her secrets and share her dreams.

A guy who wasn't him.

Jerking the door open, Mike stepped inside. Ignoring the roomful of customers sitting at the small tables, he stalked directly to the counter.

Nora's gaze snapped to his, but she managed to hide whatever she was feeling. And that worried him. Still, just looking into those blue eyes of hers was enough to convince him to stand his ground and fight for the chance to win her back.

But first things first.

Mike dropped one hand on Bill's shoulder. When the other man shot him a wary glance, Mike said shortly, "Get lost, Bill."

"What?" The man pulled away and took a step back. "You can't make me leave. This is Nora's place and I'm a customer."

All around them, people were beginning to stare. Mike felt their interested gazes but couldn't seem to care.

"The only one around here who could make me leave is Nora," Bill said.

Both men looked at her.

Nora stared at Mike. "Get lost, Bill."

Clearly disgusted, the man slapped both hands on the display case, did a quick U-turn and stormed out. In the stunned silence that followed his exit, Mike kept his gaze locked on Nora as he walked around the counter, came right up to her and took her face between his palms. He kissed her hard and long and deep, and put everything he felt, everything he'd just discovered, into the effort.

When the applause from the customers started, he broke the kiss, and ignoring the crowd, he said, "I need to talk to you."

She swayed a little, but, then, Mike's kisses always

made her a little wobbly. Add that to the complete shock of having him stride into the shop and kiss her in front of God and everyone, and was it any wonder she was a little shaky? And now he wanted to talk. Talk about what? That he wanted her? That he missed her? All good things, but she wanted more. Now she had to find out how badly Mike wanted her. She rubbed her fingers across her mouth, took a slow, deep breath and said, "So talk."

Mike glanced at the customers. "In private."

Private. When the whole town knew what had been going on between them. She glanced at the customers watching them with avid interest and then looked back at Mike. Whatever he had to say to her, he could say here. In front of witnesses. "Nope."

"No?"

Someone behind him chuckled.

Nora shook her head and stuck to her guns. "If you've got something to say to me, just say it."

Mike scraped one hand across his face, then rubbed his neck. "Not going to make this easy, are you?"

"Nothing worth having is easy, Mike," she said.

"Okay, fine." He nodded, waved one hand at the customers and said, "If you need to hear me say this in front of the whole damn town, then that's just what I'll do."

"I'm listening," she said, keeping her gaze locked on his.

"I was wrong," he blurted, figuring the best way to start was to admit the worst right up front.

"Wrong about what?"

"Hell, you name it," he muttered.

"No, Mike," she said, and tilted her head to one side, watching him carefully, "I think you should."

"You're right." He laughed shortly, shook his head and threw his hands high before letting them slap against his thighs. "Again. You were right about everything else, too."

Nora's eyes sparkled and her smile widened. That small bubble of hope that had risen in her the moment he walked into the shop now seemed to fill her heart. "So far, I like this talk."

"There's more," he promised, and reached for her. His hands came down on her shoulders, his fingers pressing into her skin, driving wedges of heat deep into every corner of her soul.

"I finally figured it out, Nora," he said, and his voice dropped to the low, husky tone that had haunted her dreams. "I need you."

Nora swallowed hard and bit down on her bottom lip to keep herself from talking. Now was the time to just listen and pray that he said what she needed to hear.

"Nothing that happened before you matters. Everything's better with you. *I'm* better with you." He rubbed his hands up and down her arms, creating a physical link between them that reached into her soul and locked on. "I *love* you, Nora."

She inhaled sharply, sweetly, and savored the words she'd hoped to hear.

"I didn't expect to—didn't want to." He shook his head and held her tighter, as if she might try to escape him. "But it's there, Nora. It's real and it's more than I ever thought I could feel."

Biting her lip was getting harder and harder. But she needed to hear one more thing, so she kept quiet.

"Marry me, Nora. Marry me and build a family with me. Be Emily's mother and help me give her brothers and sisters."

Nora released a breath she hadn't even realized she'd been holding. Suddenly, her world looked brighter. She could see the future she'd always wanted, stretching out in front of her. She looked up into those forest-green eyes of his and, for the first time, she saw love shining there. And still, she heard herself ask, "Before I answer you, I have to know, Mike. What changed your mind?"

He shot a quick glance at the people watching them, then shifted Nora to one side so that his back was to their audience and only he could see her face. "I finally understood something very simple."

"What?"

"I was...afraid to love you." He blew out a rush of breath as if admitting that had taken a lot out of

him. But once he started, he kept talking. "I was
scared to believe again. To take a chance again. And
then today I realized that if I don't take the risk, then
I'll lose you." He pulled her close and wrapped his
arms around her tightly. When she tipped her face up
to his, he said softly, "And living without you is just
not something I want to do."

"Mike, I—"

He grinned down at her. "Hey, I know what it's
cost you to be quiet for the last few minutes. But keep
it up until I can do this right, okay?"

Nora clamped her mouth shut, smiled through her
tears and nodded.

"I love you, Nora," he said, and she read the truth
in his eyes. "Will you marry me?"

"Can I talk now?"

"That depends on what you want to say."

"I want to say yes, cowboy."

That grin of his widened and her stomach did that
oh-so-familiar pitch and roll.

"Then talk, Nora."

"Yes."

His arms tightened around her as he lifted her off
her feet. "I think that's the shortest speech I've ever
heard from you."

She wrapped her arms around his neck and planted
a quick, hard kiss on his mouth. Then, smiling, she
said, "Well, don't get used to it, because I have to tell

you, it about killed me to be quiet this long when I have so much to tell you and ask you—like how's Emily and would she like to be a flower girl and—''

Mike laughed. ''You're babbling, Nora.''

''Then kiss me, cowboy. And don't you dare ever stop.''

He claimed that kiss.

And the crowd went wild.

*   *   *   *   *

Silhouette®

Desire.

presents

DYNASTIES:
THE
BARONES

An extraordinary new miniseries featuring the powerful and
wealthy Barones of Boston, an elite clan caught in a web of
danger, deceit and…desire! Follow the Barones as they overcome
a family curse, romantic scandal and corporate sabotage!

Coming March 2003, the third title of
Dynasties: The Barones:

Sleeping With
Her Rival
by Sheri WhiteFeather
(SD #1496)

A steamy "pretend" affair
turns into real love for a
determined Barone
businesswoman and the
arrogant spin doctor she's
vowed to outperform.

*Available at your
favorite retail outlet.*

Silhouette®

Where love comes alive™

Visit Silhouette at www.eHarlequin.com   SDDYNSWHR

Bestselling author

Meagan McKinney

brings you three brand-new stories in
her engaging miniseries centered around
the town of Mystery, Montana, in

MATCHED IN MONTANA

*Wedding bells always ring
when the town matriarch plays Cupid!*

Coming in February 2003:
PLAIN JANE & THE HOTSHOT, SD #1493

Coming in March 2003:
THE COWBOY CLAIMS HIS LADY, SD #1499

Coming in April 2003:
BILLIONAIRE BOSS, SD #1505

Available at your favorite retail outlet.

Where love comes alive™

Visit Silhouette at www.eHarlequin.com

SDMIM

eHARLEQUIN.com

Calling all aspiring writers!
Learn to craft the perfect romance novel
with our useful tips and tools:

- Take advantage of our **Romance Novel Critique Service** for detailed advice from romance professionals.

- Use our **message boards** to connect with writers, published authors and editors.

- Enter our **Writing Round Robin—** you could be published online!

- Learn many writing hints in our **Top 10 Writing lists!**

- **Guidelines** for Harlequin or Silhouette novels—what our editors *really* look for.

Learn more about romance writing from the experts—

visit www.eHarlequin.com today!

INTLTW

If you enjoyed what you just read,
then we've got an offer you can't resist!

Take 2 bestselling love stories FREE!

Plus get a FREE surprise gift!

Clip this page and mail it to Silhouette Reader Service™

IN U.S.A.
3010 Walden Ave.
P.O. Box 1867
Buffalo, N.Y. 14240-1867

IN CANADA
P.O. Box 609
Fort Erie, Ontario
L2A 5X3

YES! Please send me 2 free Silhouette Desire® novels and my free surprise gift. After receiving them, if I don't wish to receive anymore, I can return the shipping statement marked cancel. If I don't cancel, I will receive 6 brand-new novels every month, before they're available in stores! In the U.S.A., bill me at the bargain price of $3.57 plus 25¢ shipping and handling per book and applicable sales tax, if any*. In Canada, bill me at the bargain price of $4.24 plus 25¢ shipping and handling per book and applicable taxes**. That's the complete price and a savings of at least 10% off the cover prices—what a great deal! I understand that accepting the 2 free books and gift places me under no obligation ever to buy any books. I can always return a shipment and cancel at any time. Even if I never buy another book from Silhouette, the 2 free books and gift are mine to keep forever.

225 SDN DNUP
326 SDN DNUQ

Name _____ (PLEASE PRINT)

Address _____ Apt.#

City _____ State/Prov. _____ Zip/Postal Code

 * Terms and prices subject to change without notice. Sales tax applicable in N.Y.
** Canadian residents will be charged applicable provincial taxes and GST.
   All orders subject to approval. Offer limited to one per household and not valid to current Silhouette Desire® subscribers.
   ® are registered trademarks of Harlequin Books S.A., used under license.

DES02   ©1998 Harlequin Enterprises Limited

They weren't looking for each other...
but the chemistry was too powerful to resist.

MARY LYNN
BAXTER

A string of deadly warnings convinces Dallas mayor Jessica Kincaid to hire bodyguard Brant Harding. But as their personal agendas intersect, Jessica and Brant find themselves at odds, yet drawn to each other with a passion neither can deny. And when the threat to Jessica's life intensifies, not even Brant's best efforts may be enough to save her—or to buy them both a second chance.

HIS TOUCH

"Ms. Baxter's writing...strikes every chord within the female spirit."
—Sandra Brown

On sale February 2003
wherever paperbacks are sold!

Visit us at www.mirabooks.com

MMLB686

COMING NEXT MONTH

#1495 AMBER BY NIGHT—Sharon Sala
Amelia Beauchamp needed money, so she transformed herself from a plain-Jane librarian into a seductive siren named Amber and took a second job as a cocktail waitress. Then in walked irresistible Tyler Savage. The former Casanova wanted her as much as she wanted him, but Amelia was playing a dangerous game. Would Tyler still want her once he discovered her true identity?

#1496 SLEEPING WITH HER RIVAL—Sheri WhiteFeather
Dynasties: The Barones
After a sabotage incident left her family's company with a public-relations nightmare, Gina Barone was forced to work with hotshot PR consultant Flint Kingman. Flint decided a very public pretend affair was the perfect distraction. But the passion that exploded between Gina and heartbreakingly handsome Flint was all too real, and she found herself yearning to make their temporary arrangement last forever.

#1497 RENEGADE MILLIONAIRE—Kristi Gold
When sexy Dr. Rio Madrid learned lovely Joanna Blake was living in a slum, he did the gentlemanly thing and asked her to move in with him. But his feelings for her proved to be anything but gentlemanly—he wanted to kiss her senseless! However, Joanna wouldn't accept less than his whole heart, and he didn't know if he could give her that.

#1498 MAIL-ORDER PRINCE IN HER BED—Kathryn Jensen
Because of an office prank, shy Maria McPherson found herself being whisked away in a limousine by Antonio Boniface. But Antonio was not just any mail-order escort. He was a real prince—and when virginal Maria asked him to tutor her in the ways of love, Antonio eagerly agreed. But Maria yearned for a life with Antonio. Could she convince him to risk everything for love?

#1499 THE COWBOY CLAIMS HIS LADY—Meagan McKinney
Matched in Montana
Rancher Bruce Everett had sworn off women for good, so he was fit to be tied when stressed-out city girl Melynda Cray came to his ranch for a little rest and relaxation. Still, Melynda had a way about her that got under the stubborn cowboy's skin, and soon he was courting his lovely guest. But Melynda had been hurt before; could Bruce prove his love was rock solid?

#1500 TANGLED SHEETS, TANGLED LIES—Julie Hogan
Cole Travis vowed to find the son he hadn't known he had. His sleuthing led him to Jem—and Jem's adoptive mother, beguiling beauty Lauren Simpson. In order to find out for sure if the boy was his son, Cole posed as a handyman and offered his services to Lauren. But as Cole fell under Lauren's captivating spell…he just hoped their love would survive the truth.

SDCNM0203